I0639025

JUNCTION 1880

Steven A. Burgess

Junction 1880
Steven A. Burgess

Creative Guy Publishing | Victoria Canada

Library and Archives Canada Cataloguing in Publication

Title: Junction 1880 / Steven A. Burgess.
Other titles: Junction eighteen-eighty
Names: Burgess, Steven A., 1968- author.
Identifiers: Canadiana (print) 20200213628 | Canadiana (ebook) 20200213644 | ISBN
9781926946139   (softcover) | ISBN 9781926946146 (ebook)
Subjects: LCGFT: Novels.
Classification: LCC PS8603.U74 J86 2020 | DDC C813/.6—dc23

JUNCTION 1880

Steven A. Burgess

creative guy publishing | victoria canada

Junction 1880

Part One

CHAPTER 1

THE NOISE OF A STEAM BLAST jolted his body, knocking his head against a window and out of an unexpected nap. Disoriented, he assessed his environment, waiting as his eyes and head cleared. He was sitting on a hard wooden bench, one of many in two rows. Two or three other heads were visible sitting in front of him. He looked to his right out of a window and saw a large wooden building with the sign "Shnell's Textiles" stretched out before him. Horses with riders trotted by, a donkey with a full pack was being led at a much slower pace.

George was on the train to Junction, his home. He rubbed his head and wondered why he napped, *must have been the dinner and beer...*

The engine let out two more blasts of steam before the conductor yelled out "All aboard!" and clambered onto the train car. He leaned out of the car and peered down the platform. Seeing no further passengers, he closed the wooden door and turned, "tickets please!"

Three short whistles and the heavy *chuff* of the driving pistons started, lurching the train forward. George's body ached. He reached into his canvas bag and pulled out a ticket and his shirt, stiff and yellowed from weeks of labour. He folded the shirt into a seat cushion. He held up his ticket and looked out of the window. The train rocked and clunked over steel rails.

The bustle surrounding the wooden and brick buildings of Yorktown crept by. As the train picked up pace, the town gave way to the open prairie. Wild grasses nodded and leaned as the winds swept across. Herds of cows dotted the land, their shadows stretched by the setting sun.

The train puffed and swayed as it moved across the plains. It banged over irregularities on the roughly laid track.

Despite his pains he was content. Satisfied that weeks of hard work was going to pay off, happy with the new friends and dinner he had shared with them, pleased to be heading home.

The train pulled into the crude wood station at Junction. The rough platform caused some travelers to stumble. George clomped down the stairs exiting the train, but did not follow the others into town. Instead, he jumped off the far side of the platform and towards a split rail fence.

He tossed his canvas bag over the fence, scaled it, and followed a narrow path through the grass to a grove of poplars. The setting sun would have made the grove dark and difficult to navigate for anyone else. But George knew this path, its familiarity bringing him peace. His footfalls through the forest sounded as he knew they should, each curve and rise was as he remembered. Within a few minutes he left the trees and through the twilight saw his cabin, windows lighted and warm. The tang of wood smoke filled his nose. He arrived at the front door pulling out a large black key. He inserted it into the lock, twisted it, and the lock clunked open. He walked into the heat and shut the door as quietly as possible behind him. The latch dropped with a clink that echoed through the house.

He listened for the sound of his wife stirring. He heard nothing, but knew she was home and expecting him, as the potbellied stove in the kitchen still had fuel and was not shut down for the night. He shed his outer clothes and opened the squeaking door on the front of the stove, tossing in a chunk of hardwood. He contemplated going up to the bed located in the loft, but neither wanted to disturb his wife nor corrupt the sheets with his stench. Instead, he lay down on the bench in the main room. He had left the stove door open so that the light from the stove would color the room with flickering orange and yellow. He laid his head down on a cushion and let out a deep breath. The time for thinking and planning was done, he sank into sleep.

CHAPTER 2

GEORGE WOKE TO THE SOUND of activity outside the cabin, clanging and water splashing. *Ah*, he thought, *probably laundry*. He stood up and glanced at the kitchen table. A generous hunk of salt pork, a fresh slice of bread and a steaming mug of tea was there waiting for him!

He hurried to the kitchen table and tucked in. He contemplated the activities he needed to complete over the next few weeks while chewing on meat and sipping tea.

Maddie walked in the back door and smiled. He nodded and grinned in response, finishing his last bite of breakfast.

"Follow me," she stated. "I have a surprise for you."

George followed her out of the back door of the cabin, she led him over to a horse trough. Except the horse trough had been placed on top of a few large stones, and the smoking coals of a fire recently raked flat were underneath.

"I made you a bath," she stated.

"Wow Maddie, how did you... how... how did you get the trough over here, and doesn't the horse need it?"

"I am sure Thunder can do without his trough for a bit, and I wanted to get a lot of laundry done all at once. But first things first. You get in here—the soap, cloths and towels are here," she pointed at a crate beside the warm water. "Get yourself cleaned up and... relax a bit." Maddie walked back into the cabin.

Undressing, George looked around warily, then thought, *what am I looking for, nothing here but me and animals*. He dropped his remaining clothes and eased himself into the water. He sank into the warm depths and placed his arms on the sides. His and his wife's land was spread before him, golden grasses and poplar groves turning yellow with the start of autumn. Thunder contentedly grazed on the green grass next to Murray creek. Even the bugs weren't too bad, a combination of him being under water and a dry summer. He once more reviewed the landscape before closing his eyes, sinking into the water and soaking in the warmth.

A little while later he heard Maddie's footsteps and looked up in her direction. She looked around the area just as he had, then dropped every stitch of her clothing to the ground. George's eyebrows raised.

She reached towards the crate and grabbed a cloth, dunked it in the water and soaped it up. She began washing and rinsing herself. Once finished, she dried with one of the towels, helped along by the autumn sun and a mild prairie breeze.

She glanced into the trough and gave a wry smile, "Well, I can see you enjoyed that. If you can rinse and dry yourself in two shakes, we might partake in something else you enjoy up in the loft." She wrapped the towel around her body and skipped up to the cabin.

George was rinsed, dried, and in the cabin within two minutes.

A little while later, George stretched on the bed as Maddie finished dressing. He grinned as she pulled a sweater over her head, making her fine hair stand on end. "I want to show you something," Maddie said excitedly.

"I think I've already seen everything," teased George.

Maddie rolled her eyes, grabbed a pillow, and threw it at him. "Get your clothes on and come down." She headed down the ladder that led out of the loft. George did as he was told and followed within short order.

"Over here, over here!" Maddie gestured to the back of the cabin where the pantry was.

She opened the pantry door with a flourish, and waved her hand highlighting the sides. "Ta-da!"

All of the shelves of the pantry, floor to ceiling, were stuffed full of glass jars. Maddie pointed to one side of the pantry. "On the right side are all the sweet things: strawberry jam, blackberry jam, apple strawberry compote, Damson plum jam, and on and on! On the back and left side are all the pickled things: carrots, beans, onions, cucumbers, even a few eggs."

"Wow, very nice work!"

"I was over at Lorraine's; we spent all of last week getting us ready for winter. I always feel so much better with a fully stocked pantry. Once they are finished with the pork smoking, we can get some of that too. And there should be some dried beef coming as well. And, Oh! Here we have my half of a twenty-pound keg of Darjeeling tea, imported from India! Lorraine and I decided to treat ourselves, and when you buy this much, it's not any more than regular tea, really."

"My mouth is watering already, and so well organized, looking forward to the fresh toast and jam and apple pies; thank you!"

"You are more than welcome." Maddie considered for a moment, "So what are your plans for today?"

"Well, I have a couple of things to pick up at Service Mercantile, and I need to meet JJ out at his place. You?"

"So you will need the horse and wagon?"

"Yes."

"Then I will get them ready, and I am coming with you." She smiled. "While I am getting ready, can you take your clothes from your trip and wash them in the bath water outside? All the laundry stuff is in its usual place."

George suppressed a sigh and nodded. "Will do."

Maddie closed the pantry door and headed out the back of the cabin towards the horse shelter. George followed, heading towards an open-sided storage lean-to located just behind the cabin. He grabbed a washboard and put it beside the bath. He then lugged a laundry wringer back to the bath as well. Laundry wasn't work that George enjoyed, but he supposed it wasn't work that anyone really enjoyed. He dumped the canvas bag of clothes into the warm water, and after brief consideration, threw the bag in as well. He pulled out each piece of clothing, rubbed it with soap, pushed it underwater soaking thoroughly, then scrubbed it on the washboard, He was careful not to scrub his knuckles, having learned that painful lesson numerous times already. He watched with satisfaction the yellow and other stains come out.

He put each piece through the double-rolled laundry wringer, rolling it through using the crank on the side, and allowed them to drop into a washtub. This was followed by a trip to the stream for rinsing, and another go through the laundry wringer.

He had just started putting his clothes up on the drying line strung between the cabin and storage shelter when he heard the sound of horse hooves, the rattle of a harness, and the squeak of wagon wheels behind him. Maddie set the wagon brake, hopped off the cart, and they both hung the rest of the laundry.

"Horse looks good," commented George as they both got onto the wagon.

"Thunder always looks great after a brushing, and he enjoys it so." Maddie replied. George nodded.

Maddie grabbed the reigns and with a quick "Ha"—and flip—they were on their way to town.

CHAPTER 3

THE WAGON BUMPED OVER the train tracks, Thunder led by Maddie's practiced hand. George had replaced the wooden seat with a carriage seat, providing some relief from the bumps due to its built-in springs and cushioning. They headed down the main street of Junction.

Maddie commented, "I really like the town's look since they put in the new boardwalk. It makes it more grown-up somehow, like a real town. And nice not to have to step in the mud."

George agreed as he noticed the local saloon, *Sticky Pete's*, and hoped he could play some poker there later.

"Where did you say this place was?" asked Maddie.

"On the other side of Robert and Lorraine's. JJ has a quarter section up next to the Blue Hills."

Maddie made the appropriate adjustment to their course as they left town, and asked, "So, your time in Yorktown; how did it go?"

George considered. "Well, I arrived at the station just before lunch, and headed over to Smith and Son's Doors and Windows. I walked around the block, taking a look at the place, and noticed they kept the glass outside around back. Not covered, but glass doesn't mind rain I suppose."

Maddie nodded. "Sure."

"And, under cover, they kept some nice straight, seasoned lumber, good-quality stuff. It looked like the main workshop was on the ground floor of the building, and maybe an office upstairs."

"Did you just walk in?" Maddie asked.

"They had an 'experienced labour wanted' poster out front, very fortuitous."

"Very," said Maddie.

"I noticed the workers were just leaving the workshop." George paused as they went over a bump. Thunder snorted and continued. George leaned back on the plush seat. "They were outside for lunch, so I headed over, and met the crew and Alex, the foreman. I introduced myself by handing out some of your Damson plums."

"They are tasty," Maddie agreed.

"We talked about Yorktown, the railroad, the summer weather, and making windows, of course. So finished up lunch with them and headed up to the office. It was on the second floor; I knocked on the door. I waited a bit, then someone said, 'In!'

"Opened the door and saw the office was pretty sparse, not like the office at Shnell's Textiles, and not even close to a banker's office. I assumed this meant that the boss was focused on saving money and efficiency."

"Okay," said Maddie.

"He motioned me to a chair in front of his desk and told me to sit, which I did.

"'Name's John. Here for a job?'

"'Yes sir.'

"'You have experience working with wood?'

"'Yes, eighteen years. I have been working as a journeyman for ten, and was head carpenter at Shnell's Textiles.'

"John's eyebrows raised. 'I'm not paying journeyman's wages here; we aren't made of money. I hate to waste your time.' He motioned to the door.'

"'Oh, I'm not looking for money.'

"John was again surprised.

"'I want to work for some windows.'

"'Ahh,' said John, 'you have your eyes on some of our deluxe bay windows but can't quite get the cash together right now?'

"'Just the opposite; in fact, I want forty of your smallest windows. I can work for six weeks.'

"John leaned back in his chair looking skeptical. He stared at me for a while, then scratched something on a paper.

"'Forty windows is way too many; there is no way we can put aside that many hours for something we make no money on.'

"'I'm asking for the two-foot-by-two-foot windows. You know, the ones that you don't have to change the jigs for; with three sets of jigs you can probably get those done in half a day. You have done pretty close to that before with a smaller crew than you have now.'

"John looked surprised again. Before he could interject, I said, 'I know the panes you use in those windows are only eight by eight, so that's leftover glass from many of your other projects.'

"John frowned and his voice went low. 'You seem to have a lot of knowledge about my business.'

"I nodded, 'Yep, had lunch with your boys downstairs.'

"John looked annoyed, even slightly angry."

"Maybe he didn't like being told about his business," said Maddie.

"Not many men do," replied George.

"But you got the job?" asked Maddie.

"I said, 'Look, I know you have a big order for the new hotel due in five weeks. If you hire me, with the guys you have now, you can make that order. Or, I can walk out of that door and you can take your chances with whoever happens upon this place next. Up to you.'

"John sighed. And thought. And in a very final tone, he said, 'Here is the deal. *If* we make the five-week deadline, you will get your windows built on the last day here. And it will not be forty windows—thirty-six—two foot by two foot.' He held out his hand. 'Don't make me wait.'

"I stood up and shook his hand." George turned to Maddie. "And tomorrow, we get the shipment of brand new windows!"

Maddie nodded. "Good. All thanks to my Damson plums." She grinned at George, turned the wagon off of the main cart trail and headed past Robert and Lorraine's farm at a slower pace to accommodate the irregularities of the prairie.

"Now, this JJ guy, how did you meet him?"

"Did you want the full story or a quick version?" asked George.

Maddie shrugged. "We have almost half an hour till we get there; how about the full story." Maddie had missed George over the last six weeks. At first, it was nice to do things around the house without having to consider another person to feed, clean up after, or coordinate with. After a few days, though, she started to miss his company, the constant bustle of his various projects and updates to their homestead. His conversation. And his presence at night provided some comfort from the strange sounds of the wilderness.

George drew in a deep breath and thought about the foreman at the window factory, Alex. He looked over the fields they were passing— the clear sky, the freshly trampled and scalloped wheat with upright bundles ripening in the sun. He sensed hardwood smoke from pork smoking along with other farm sounds and smells.

He thought about the tenement buildings that Alex lived in. The smell of sweat and dirty clothes. Children playing and shouting, constant human noises, loud talking—even arguing— dishes and pans clanking. And the stench of questionable sanitation.

Alex and George had gotten along famously the first afternoon they worked, with lots of good stories and a shared understanding of wood and accomplishment that gained mutual respect.

"Alex invited me over to his house to stay while I was in town," stated George.

"After knowing you for only one day?" said Maddie in amazement.

"I hope you get to meet Alex, Maddie; he is a warm and generous man with so much positivity and spirit, he can find the good side of any situation."

Maddie nodded and navigated the wagon around a small drainage ditch.

"So we walked up to his front door, narrowly being missed by someone upstairs discarding dirty water. Chamber pot water."

Maddie wrinkled her nose.

"Then Alex said: 'Welcome to my palace!' We walked in the main door to the building, past a staircase and some other doors, until we reached his apartment. He opened the door and walked straight into the kitchen where his wife was. She did not look happy to see me. And then Alex said, 'This is George our new expert window maker, and he is staying with us for six weeks!'

"She was even less impressed at this point. She grabbed Alex's hand and towed him to another room in the back."

Maddie leaned in, listening closer.

"I couldn't hear much, but the gist was easy to make out. I heard my name, I heard six weeks; I heard their two kids' and JJ's names. The kids were sitting at the table in the kitchen looking uncomfortably at their soup.

"She stormed back out and headed straight for me. I reached in my pocket and pulled out a thin bundle of fivers. I held them up for her. 'This is the money I had put aside for room and board this trip, it's not much, ten bucks a week. I would much rather you have it than a hotel.'

"She took the money and counted it carefully. And smiled.

"She said, 'Pull up a chair, Mr. Wainwright. Happy to have you. We have a chamber pot for liquids and you can head out to the back for the other. You're staying in the kids' room.'

"The kids did not look impressed. And that was that!" stated George.

Maddie chuckled and paused for a moment. "So, this JJ; he is the person we are going to see now?"

"Yes, we were introduced at dinner—potato and onion soup—and he seemed like a quiet and solid fellow. Wasn't sure of his relation to Alex, he didn't look related."

The wagon creaked and bumped through the grasses, Thunder's tail swished away the occasional fly.

"And," said Maddie, "JJ?"

"Right," stated George. "About a week later, the three of us were standing outside for Alex's and JJ's before-bed tobacco break."

Maddie looked disgusted.

"Believe me," said George, "the smell of tobacco was a nice break from a lot of the other smells there. JJ looked nervous; he kept looking at his feet.

"'You gonna ask him, JJ?' said Alex. JJ looked like he wanted to say something but when he looked in my eyes he quickly looked away."

"'Then I will.' stated Alex.

"'JJ is a trapper. He lives up close to where you live; he has a quarter section over by the blue hills. A couple of problems have left him in a tricky spot,' Alex said carefully. 'He was coming back from his trap lines this spring when the ice gave way on the Blue River. He lost his pack with his traps that he had just collected.'

"'And the three pelts I had just got.' added JJ, looking suddenly embarrassed.

"'So he came to Yorktown to earn some money, including a week or so at Smith and Son's. But JJ has trouble keeping a schedule.'

"'In the country, the woods and sky wake you up, and if you're tired you occasionally sleep in.' JJ stated defiantly.

"'So JJ wasn't able to earn much,' nodded Alex, 'and had to spend what he did earn on just living, no room for savings.'"

George stated to Maddie, "So I suddenly knew why JJ was staying with them, and why his wife was mad to see me. She thought he had brought in someone else who needed help."

George continued, "So Alex says: 'JJ would really like to get back out to his trapping lines.'

"JJ said, 'I just ain't built for the city, not even close.' He shook his head emphatically."

Maddie said, "So you lent him some money."

George nodded. "My last ten bucks, but I already had a return train ticket and room and board, so didn't need it.

"JJ was so happy and appreciative! He looked at the ten bucks and said, 'I can get a dozen new traps for this, maybe even a gun and some ammo! Thank you!'"

George finished, "He gave my hand a hearty shake, and that was that."

"And that was that," replied Maddie, "and this is this," she said, pointing out a canvas shelter nestled at the bottom of the hills.

"And this is this!" replied George.

"This place reminds me of Junction when we first arrived; remember that, George?"

"I do; nothing but a train station, Service Mercantile, and about a hundred of those tents. Mostly labourers."

Maddie nodded. "So glad to be out of the noise and the muck!"

"It was definitely great motivation for getting the cabin built on our section. And winter was on its way too."

"Thank goodness for the late winter that year, didn't really show up 'till late September," replied Maddie. She pulled the wagon up to the front of the canvas tent. Stretching racks with freshly processed skins stood out front. She locked the wheels with a firm pull of the wooden wheel lock.

CHAPTER 4

GEORGE WALKED TOWARDS THE TENT. "You coming?" he asked Maddie.

"Not right now. Thunder was acting a bit jumpy just after the farm, so I am going to stay and settle him a bit." She jumped down from the wagon and, while speaking with soothing tones, rubbed Thunder's neck and nose.

"Is that you George?" boomed a voice from inside the tent.

"It sure is!" replied George.

"I'll be right out!" There was shuffling in the tent, the clank of metal and the rustle of chains. More movement, some grunting, and a question—"You want some sage tea? Just brewed it up this morning."

George thought a moment. "Sure, sounds great."

JJ opened the flap on the front of his tent and gave George a warm welcome, "Well, there you are! Good to see you, my man." JJ gave George a hearty handshake with a robust back pat.

"And you brought the little woman!" JJ exclaimed, taking a few quick strides over to Maddie. When Maddie unconsciously stepped back, JJ extended his hand for a handshake. "Have heard a lot about you lady, all good." JJ smiled broadly.

Maddie replied, "I should hope so too, I *am* an amazing woman." All three laughed.

JJ turned to Maddie. "Tea?"

Maddie agreed.

JJ disappeared back into his tent before emerging with two aromatic steaming mugs. "This will take the chill out of you," as he handed the mugs to them.

He turned to George, but resumed speaking to Maddie.

"This man," he said, "lent me ten dollars when few would!" He gave George a pat on the shoulder. He turned to see Maddie nodding.

"And the trapping has been good! Just pulled up my first line yesterday, can't take too many from one area, as they gotta make more. " He winked at George.

"Lots of rabbits, of course—not complaining— good eats and good for clothes. But also two beavers and even an ermine! Speaking of which..." JJ again disappeared into the tent.

Maddie and George sipped their tea in silence.

"I have something for you," JJ came out of the tent. He handed George a tin full of coins. "Glad to give it to you, not only to pay you back, but I hate having cash in the tent, attracts the wrong kind of attention." George emptied the coins into his pocket and handed back the tin.

"George," said JJ. "I heard a rumour back at Junction."

"Oh boy," said George.

"They said you don't hunt, George? You don't even own a rifle?" JJ paused, studying him.

George sipped and thought. "I don't like rumours, too much trouble."

JJ looked uncomfortable. Maddie looked at George.

"But I consider you a friend JJ, so I will clear this up. It's true. I don't hunt."

JJ shrugged. "Okay." He considered. "Why?"

George sighed. "Well, a couple of reasons really. First off, I am nearsighted. Not real bad. I can see pretty clearly up to ten yards, then things turn into blurry shapes, the further they are, the worse. So, at a hundred yards, I can't tell the difference between a cow and a buffalo. And I certainly can't pick a deer out of deep woods."

JJ nodded. "Glasses?"

"They don't make glasses for what I have."

"Oh." another pause. "You said there was a couple of reasons."

"Well, to be completely honest, in some tense situations, I freeze up. When I first moved to Junction, I got invited by the sheriff and a few boys to go hunting. We had just moved to town, so I recognized that this was a way to get acquainted. Was hoping honestly that we didn't run into anything. They loaned me a Winchester rifle."

JJ focused on George.

"Well, it was more like something ran into me. The group had spotted a few deer in a clearing in the woods, so they spread out and tried to get a shot at a buck. I laid low, so low in fact, that the deer did not see me. I heard shouting, 'Take a shot, George!' so I stood up.

"The deer were startled, me popping up out of the shrubbery, and they bolted in different directions. A young deer, hadn't even lost all of her spots, charged me. I didn't want to shoot a fawn, but realized later that I probably could have shot in the air to startle it. I could probably have moved out of the way too. Instead I watched frozen as the animal lowered its head and butted me at full speed right in the stomach. I hit the ground gasping for air; most of the guys I was with were laughing at me being taken out by a fawn. I wasn't embarrassed at first, but was once I got my breath back."

"Wow," said JJ, "Uh... Wow."

"So I was the butt of quite a few jokes for the next couple of years. 'Lookout George, there's a squirrel, he may charge,' and, 'Dive George, that bunny's going to take you out.' I got used to it. I didn't get invited to go hunting again."

"That is a sad, sad tale," said JJ, shaking his head slowly with a small smile on his face. All three started laughing again.

"Well, I have to go set these new traps. Hair trigger on these, much less escaping," JJ said. He headed back into the shelter and came out with his jingling pack. "Throw those cups in the door when you're done, Thanks."

JJ wandered away and called back, "Watch out for charging gophers!" He laughed again, Maddie gave George pat on the back.

"He couldn't resist," said George.

"You Okay?" she asked.

"Oh yeah. Let's head back to town, got some money to spend."

"One of my favourite activities," said Maddie.

They tucked their empty cups back in the shelter and got on the wagon. Maddie turned the wagon and they headed down the same cart tracks they had just cut into the ground. The wagon bumped and squeaked its way across the prairie.

"That sage tea was pretty good," noted George. He noticed she had finished the cup.

"It was," she said while concentrating on steering Thunder. "I will have to ask JJ, or if you see him first, ask him what was in it."

George said sarcastically. "Uh, sage?"

Maddie shook her head. "That wasn't just sage, George; there were other things in there. I think maybe some wild mint. There was something almost like menthol. It was most refreshing, cleared out the breathing."

George nodded.

"And George," Maddie added. "I really do appreciate the carriage seat in this, takes the bumps out but..." Maddie bounced and squeaked the seat. "Do you think you could maybe... oil the springs?"

George chuckled. "Sure, sure."

They approached the farm as they had on the trip out. The farm was on the left; a grove of hardwoods on the right, the same side as Maddie.

"Thunder, easy. Easy!" Maddie pulled on the reigns. "Thunder is acting up again." Maddie focused on keeping a firm hand on the reigns and using calming language. "Easy boy."

George looked with interest at the horse's head. The animal kept looking to the right, and his ears had both pivoted to a distant point. George followed the ears and saw something. Sprinting at the edge of the grove was a tawny-brown shape. George's spine crackled with realization. He couldn't make out what it was, but its pace and intent were obvious. It was running at the cart! Its sinewy form was moving with a terrifying efficiency.

George knew with certainty that this animal was after Maddie. An adrenaline rush surged through his body. He felt a rage build inside, a fury that his wife was the target of such an attack. His next motions happened without conscious thought.

He cried out "NOOOOO!" and leaned forward. He flipped open the front door of a wooden storage trunk located under the seat. It felt like the air itself was resisting him. He grasped the shotgun stored inside, sat up and twisted right. He pushed Maddie forward. If not for her feet planted on the buckboard, she would have flipped over the front of the wagon.

He leaned his right elbow against the back of the seat, Thunder's pulling and straining made a clear shot very difficult. He pulled back one of the hammers on the shotgun, put his finger on front trigger, and looked up. A snarling face appeared.

He saw teeth and eyes: lips curled back over white teeth, yellow narrowed eyes. Two powerful paws raised high with claws extended. He pulled the trigger—a blast of powder and shot left the gun.

Thunder cried out in fear and attempted to bolt. He pulled full strength for a hundred yards, the cart nearly turning on its side a number of times. Maddie had righted herself and was trying to gain control of the bouncing and jolting wagon. George flipped over the back of the seat and landed in the back. He attempted to grab the sides but was shaken off.

Thunder started bucking, his front legs planting and back legs kicking. His head jerked side to side as he attempted to free himself from the wagon. His back leg fell outside the right trace, and the new sensation in his groin made him go wild. Powerful feet, twisting black body coated with sweat, cries of fear warbling out of his foaming mouth. Maddie held on.

Thunder's rear leg landed on the right trace snapping it. He twisted and bucked, yanking hard against the other trace. That trace ripped out of its anchor, Thunder was off at full gallop, traces and reigns flying behind him. Maddie cried out, "THUNDER!" and leapt off the cart and sprinted after him.

CHAPTER 5

GEORGE'S FIRST CONCERN WAS the cougar. He grabbed the shotgun and stood up in the back of the wagon. He could see Maddie still running, Thunder growing smaller with every stride.

He did a sweep of the area, his blurry vision doing the best it could to spot any movement. He didn't know if he had wounded the animal or missed it. Unable to spot anything, he climbed off the back of the wagon, shotgun in hand, and retraced the cart's path back through the grass.

His nerves still humming, he pulled back on the second hammer of the shotgun and placed his finger on the second trigger. His steps crunched in the dry grass. As he approached the initial point of attack, he saw a brown form settled in the grass. Raising the shotgun, he approached.

He saw powerful haunches and a thick tail resting in the grass. He circled it. It was not going to move again. His shot had removed half of the animals face, flies already alighting on the glistening surface.

He felt profound sorrow. George walked up beside the cougar, squatted down, and placed his hand upon the fur. It was still warm. Tears welled up in his eyes.

"I am so sorry that this had to happen." Drops ran down his nose and dripped onto the ground below. "But you were after my wife.

And I cannot let you take Maddie from me. YOU TRIED TO TAKE MADDIE FROM ME!" He bowed his head and sobbed.

He did not hear the horses galloping hooves until they were just behind him. Dolly, one of the farmer's children, galloped by at full speed in the direction of Maddie and Thunder. Lorraine pulled up within twenty yards with her horse, got down and pulled a Remington rifle out from its sheath on the horse. She lowered the rifle and pointed it at the carcass, walking forward.

"You won't need that Lorraine," George released the hammer on his gun and placed it in the grass. Lorraine looked at the animal's face and understood.

Tears still on his face, George looked at Lorraine. "He tried to take Maddie! I couldn't let that happen. I have never heard of an animal trying to take someone off of a cart. Never in my life!"

Lorraine looked away from George, and to his surprise, knelt by the dead animal. Although silent, George could tell by the movement of her shoulders and head that she was crying.

George felt both confusion and great empathy. He knelt down beside her and rubbed between her shoulder blades.

Lorraine confided, "Ten years ago we had first settled this area, before Junction, before the surveyors and track labourers, before anyone else. My sister and daughter were riding back from a day of gathering rose hips, wild onions, and any edible berries they could find." Lorraine took a deep breath. "Dolly was only six at the time, a slight young thing compared to today. A cougar must have been hiding in the deep grass because it ambushed Dolly, knocking her off the horse.

"My sister, as any mother would, immediately jumped off her horse and took on the cougar trying to drag Dolly back into the grass. She jumped onto the cougar, and he, surprised by the attack, released Dolly. She screamed, 'Go back to the farm, go back to the farm!'" Lorraine paused.

"I knew later that my sister was dead. The way her body hung off the back of Robert's horse, the look on his face."

Lorraine started sobbing. George, sensing it was time, stood up. Lorraine also stood up, dried her eyes, and brushed off her front.

"We have raised Dolly ever since as one of our own." She glared at George. "As far as anyone knows, Dolly is our daughter and it will remain that way." George nodded, understanding. Lorraine let out a combined laugh and cry.

"Yes, George, I have heard of a cougar attacking..." Her voice cracked. "And trying to take someone off a horse." She looked in the direction of her daughter's gallop. "What's taking those two so long?"

George picked up his gun, and motioned to Lorraine. They both walked back to the wagon. She looked at his gun. "I don't know of many who would cut down a gun like that."

"We don't use it for hunting... It's purely for defence. It's pretty hard to miss with a shortened barrel like this, when things are close."

"I can see that," said Lorraine.

George climbed into the back of the wagon and looked in the direction of Thunder's gallop. "I think I can see them." He saw two shapes—the black of Thunder, and the light brown of Spirit. "They are walking."

Lorraine looked visibly relieved. "Thunder is probably too wound up for riding."

George trudged back over to the cougar. Lorraine leaned against the wagon, looked at the sky, and let out a sigh. George glanced down at the cougar, sat, and waited.

A little while later, Maddie and Dolly walked up with the horses, and had a brief conversation with Lorraine that George could not hear. Lorraine stayed with Maddie and Dolly mounted Spirit, taking just a few short canters to get to where George was sitting. She saw the cougar and her eyes grew wide. She dismounted Spirit and gave him a rub on the neck. She walked over to the limp form on the ground and looked at it.

"Look at the size of that thing. You shot it?" George nodded. "It looks so peaceful right now." She paused. "Except for the missing face." Dolly gave her head a little shake. "Its paws are huge! They look like oven mitts! " She knelt down and gently took one in her hand. She pushed on one of its pads, a large white claw extended.

"Wow," she said. "Are you going to keep it?"

George hadn't even considered it.

Dolly stated, "I mean, you shot it, so it is yours. But it's not much of a trophy like this." She wrinkled her nose. "If you're not going to keep it, I would love to have it, I mean, if that's okay."

"Dolly, mind your manners!" Lorraine and Maddie had walked up behind.

"Give the man a chance to breathe and don't go asking for things without..." she trailed off.

George stood up. "It's okay. You can have it, Dolly. Don't think cougar is even good eating though."

Lorraine explained, "It's actually not bad, a bit like really lean pork. You need to add a lot of fat to fry them, or it's fine in stews. Makes a change from the usual anyway. Thank you, George, we will make sure that nothing goes to waste."

George managed a weak smile. "Is it okay if we leave the cart here for a while; we need to get Thunder home and calm first, probably will head out first thing with some tools to pick it up?"

"Of course," said Lorraine.

They left, Maddie holding Thunder's reigns in one hand, and George's hand in the other.

CHAPTER 6

THE WALK HOME WAS LONG, dry, and mostly silent. George and Maddie had to walk around the town limits, as Junction, like most towns in the area, had a strict no-gun law. George had kept his shotgun, not wanting to leave it unattended in his broken cart for an unknown period.

They walked up the remainder of the dusty trail to their cabin, Maddie passed Thunder's reigns to George. "Can you settle him in?" she asked, heading straight for the cabin. This was unusual, as Maddie usually enjoyed settling Thunder. George took Thunder over to their small barn, and put him in the first of two stalls. He forked in some hay and hung a quarter bucket of oats from the corner post. Normally Thunder would have pushed his nose straight in and started eating the oats, but tonight he simply stood, tail swishing.

George took two metal buckets down to the creek and filled both. He walked back up to the barn and splashed the cool water into Thunder's trough. Thunder took a couple of steps towards the trough and lowered his head until his nose was just above the water. He let out a couple of snorts, lowered his mouth into the water, and started drinking. Lightly at first, then deep gulps. George went down to the creek and got two more buckets of water.

After Thunder had finished drinking, he wandered over to the oat bucket, lowered his head, and started chewing. George walked up beside him.

"Quite a day, hey buddy?" George brushed the animal, his coat matted with dirt and sweat. Thunder's skin quivered as George ran the brush over it. After brushing, he checked Thunder's legs by rubbing them down gently but could find no signs of injury. The traces had left some abrasions in his groin, but nothing that didn't look like it could heal.

George decided he would take him down to the livery tomorrow for an expert opinion and possible treatment, and then the blacksmith to check on his shoes.

George placed the brush back on the bench outside of the two stalls, and quietly closed the barn door.

He stepped inside the cabin, and was somewhat alarmed to see Maddie sitting on the eating bench, staring at the blank wall. From the look of her clothes and shoes, she hadn't moved since she came in. He walked over and touched her shoulder. "Maddie?" Maddie twitched away from his hand.

George considered. "You okay?" Maddie's legs started vibrating, thighs and calves twitching. Then her stomach, upper body and finally her arms. Her teeth started chattering. George walked to the back of the cabin and grabbed a blanket. He placed it over Maddie's shoulders, she grabbed the corners to pull it in close.

She continued shaking, sometimes making a chattering *ah-ah-ah-ah-ah* sound. George walked over to the potbellied stove and put in a couple of pieces of hardwood. He stoked the fire until orange flames started up the side of the logs. He placed a kettle full of water on the top of the stove.

He walked over to Maddie, and, without touching her, sat down beside her. She continued to shake for a good while, until she let out a low moan, and the shaking tapered off. Once she had stopped, George asked, "You want to go to bed?"

Maddie gave a quick small nod, and George held out his arm. She grabbed it, and they headed back to the ladder that led to the loft. George stood at the bottom of the ladder, hands up, ready to catch her if she slipped. She didn't, and clambered into bed. She grabbed the top blanket, wrapped herself in it, shoes and dirty clothes still on, and lay still.

George went back to the dining area intent on making tea. Now that Maddie had gone to bed however, he felt heavy and tired. He took the kettle off the stove, closed the vents, and locked the cabin doors. He headed up to the attic, took off his sweaty, dusty clothes, and climbed in bed. He lay there silently for a moment, finding some soothing and peace in the rhythm of Maddie's breathing.

He had just fallen asleep when white glistening teeth and yellow, narrowed eyes jolted his body awake. He let out a deep breath,

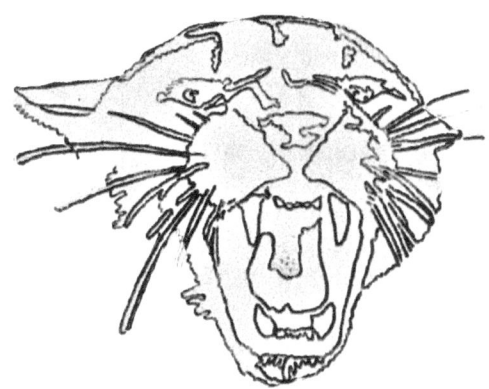

let the image fade, and looked at the ceiling until he again fell asleep.

The next morning, George woke to the brightness of sunshine streaming in through the small attic window. He listened for the sound of his wife breathing. Not hearing it, he reached across the bed to confirm she wasn't there. At first worried, he then detected the smell of wood smoke, and heard the quiet clanking and sounds of movement downstairs. He lay still for a while, allowing these sounds to comfort him.

As he was getting dressed, he heard another familiar sound. It was the clomping of horse hooves outside on the dry ground, and a rhythmic squeaking that sounded a lot like the seat on their wagon. He got the rest of his clothes on and went down.

Maddie was already outside. George looked out and saw Lorraine and his wagon being pulled by Mort, the powerful workhorse that powered most of the equipment on Lorraine and Robert's farm.

"Lorraine!" exclaimed Maddie. "Did not expect to see you here!"

Lorraine smiled and nodded slightly. "Well, we couldn't just leave your wagon out by our farm overnight, so we got old Mort here to pull it in yesterday after you left."

George gave a quick wave and smile, and walked up to Mort. George had always appreciated Mort; he was a quiet, calm workhorse that never complained and steadily went about his business. George inhaled the strong smell of Mort, walked beside him, and gave his neck a rub. Mort lowered his head and gave a short neigh. He then started nudging George's body at his hips. "Sorry buddy, no oats in my pocket today."

Mort's best attribute was also sometimes a source of frustration. He took a great deal of convincing to move faster than a walk; nobody ever went anywhere fast riding Mort.

Lorraine stated, "You and that horse have a bit of a bond I think. He doesn't react like that to most people."

"I like Mort, too." George paused. "Thank you so much for bringing the wagon, and fixing the traces, I thought things would need much more fixing after that ride!"

"We did too," stated Lorraine, "but once we got the wagon back to the barn and gave it a good looking over, the only problem was the broken trace and the wagon connection with the other trace. You made some customizations to the wagon that made it tougher than it looks, a bit of hardwood here in key parts, metal reinforcement on the corners. I think Robert was actually impressed, although he would never tell you that." Lorraine winked.

"Well thanks again," said Maddie. "Can you bring the wagon over by the barn and we will unhitch Mort?"

"Sure can," said Lorraine, "And I brought the riding gear for the old guy; we can get that on and I can head back. Farming's never done!"

They both headed over to the barn and George went back inside for his tea and breakfast.

CHAPTER 7

MADDIE HAD TAKEN THUNDER out of the barn and was leading him around the yard, talking gently and occasionally rubbing his neck. George slowly walked up so as not to spook the animal and looked at Maddie.

"That was nice of Lorraine and Robert to fix up and bring back the wagon."

"Very nice," replied Maddie.

"I don't suppose there is any chance he can pull that wagon today?" George asked.

"I don't think that's a good idea," replied Maddie. "I am going to take him down to the livery and get him looked over, and to the blacksmith to check on his shoes. I want him to otherwise have a calm day. If he is still calm for all of today, we can test-hook him up to the wagon tomorrow, and see his reaction. He needs time."

George nodded. "Of course." He sighed.

"I know that sigh," said Maddie.

"I have a load of windows due at the station this morning, and Claude, well, he..."

"I know Claude," said Maddie. "But he will just have to wait. We don't have an option on this, and pushing Thunder when he is not ready means it will take that much longer to get him back in front of the wagon."

"I know. I know... Thank you."

George headed down the path to Junction. Maddie watched for a moment, and continued walking Thunder around the yard. George walked the dry path through the poplar grove past their house, his boots crunching on the dry leaves. The air inside the forest was colder and fresher; he enjoyed it as it helped clear his thoughts. After leaving the edge of the forest, he walked towards the train station visible in the distance.

Getting closer, he could see a load on the station platform that was most likely his windows. Mostly he felt relieved that this part of the delivery had been completed, but also anticipated what was coming...

"Where is your wagon!" demanded Claude, the stationmaster, sensing something was up.

"There has been a bit of a complication," replied George.

"There is always a fucking complication!" exclaimed Claude. "I work my skin to the bone keeping this station in good running order, every day, no fail, and every day, someone just like you screws it up. Let's hear it, what is your sorry excuse? Your mother is dead? Your cabin burned down? Your horse is lame?" Claude's face and bulbous nose were red and sweaty with the exertion of his outburst.

"Thunder went outside the traces yesterday. The wagon is fine, Thunder just needs a day to calm down before..."

"I am going outside the fucking traces!" screamed Claude. "Do you think this station platform is a storage site for your convenience?

Do you think, when the next load comes in, I appreciate all your shit in the way? And GLASS too! So we have to take extra care not to bump it, or you will fill out some bullshit insurance claim and make my life WORSE. Every day I come into this place with a smile on my face, and every day some new bullshit screws that up, and I keep coming back. I think, what is wrong with me, why do I keep doing this—tell me, George, why do I keep doing this?"

George said nothing.

"You say nothing, because there is no excuse," Claude continued his rant, his face inches from George, flecks of spit flying out and hitting George's face. George let Claude rant until he had run out of steam.

"Going to poker this Thursday?" asked George.

"It's fucking Thursday, isn't it! Of course I am going to poker!" replied Claude.

"If you can hold my windows for the night"— Claude's eyes bulged—"I will buy all the beer you can drink for poker night."

George knew this was not a cheap proposition. For a small man, Claude could put away serious quantities of alcohol. Claude straightened up and dropped his shoulders a little. "Deal," he said, extending his hand. George shook it and left before any further discussion could occur.

He walked over to the track crossing, a crude assemblage of rough-hewn wood placed over the tracks, worn and battered with the weight of wagons bringing goods from the station. He stood at the centre of the crossing, and listened carefully for the sound of any approaching train.

He heard nothing. The warm sun was on his face, the smell of wood preservative from the railroad ties filled his nose. An occasional gust of wind brought the smell of dried grass and animals from the livery.

He looked straight down Main Street from the crossing and chuckled as he saw the distinct form of Mort in the distance plodding back to the farm. He remembered watching this town grow from dozens of tents. Service Mercantile was one of the first buildings, followed by the Sheriff's Office and the first stage of Sticky Pete's saloon. It had grown from a small but always-crowded drinking house to an impressive building with rooms for let on the second floor, and a sweeping, curved veranda on the front two sides that were often interspersed with beer and whiskey drinkers watching the trains and passersby.

He looked down the track towards Yorktown, and remembered the pace and smells of the city. It was not a place he felt comfortable, but he had made good friends there. And he could always find work there when local jobs were thin. He turned and looked up the track the other way, where it split into two tracks. One headed north, where its main function was bringing back the wood harvested from the vast northern pine forests. The other headed south west, towards the coal mines and lime mining operations that fed the industries of Yorktown.

Giving his head a small shake to bring himself back to the present, he headed down the main street of Junction and stopped in front of a freshly leveled and prepared building site. There was a load of lumber, just dropped off in the last couple of days. And the foundation for the building, as well as a river-rock wall extending around the building foundation were just finished. He took a closer look at the rock wall, wondering if the lime from one of the mines had been used for the mortar. He squatted down and squinted, looking across the top of the rock wall. It was straight and true. Impressed, George silently saluted the craftsmanship of the stonemasons.

He then walked over to the lumber pile, lifted one of the planks and looked down its length. It was straight, true, and well planed. He again contemplated the stone masons' skills and...

"YOU THERE!" a voice shouted out behind him.

A tall thin bald man with upright posture and a blue vest with shiny brass buttons strode towards him. "*What* do you think you're doing!"

George could not imagine a man who looked more out of place.

"Unhand that wood!" the man stated.

George put the plank down. "This is some very well-seasoned and processed lumber," George volunteered, "and the foundation..."

"I do not need the opinion of some random stranger about these building supplies," the man blustered.

George extended his hand, introducing himself. "George Wainwright."

The man looked distinctly unimpressed. "Thank you for your name, I now know who to look for if the wood goes missing." He raised his chin and looked down at George with suspicion.

George's normally expressive face froze. He thought for an uncomfortably long moment. Just as the man started to walk away, he asked, "You haven't been to the telegraph office in the last few days, have you?" The man froze, but did not turn or say a word. "I am going to be at Sticky Pete's for the next few hours, if you're looking for me," stated George. "The telegraph office is located in the station."

The man turned briefly and sneered at George "I know where the telegraph office is." He turned briskly and walked away, not in the direction of the telegraph office.

George sighed, then started walking back in the direction of Sticky Pete's. He decided that he was going to have a breakfast beer.

CHAPTER 8

WHEN GEORGE WALKED IN through the swinging gates at the entrance to Sticky Pete's, he didn't raise his hands to push them, or even raise his arms to move them out of his way, he simply allowed his body weight to move them aside. He took a brief look around, marvelling at the wear the floor showed from four years of hard use, a floor he had built.

Two locals were playing pool at the back of the establishment, the occasional crack of billiard balls echoing off the wooden walls. A young couple were sharing coffee and a quiet but intense conversation in the front area. Brad, the local blacksmith, was drinking coffee at the bar. Brad was a mountain of a man; the coffee cup looked comically small in his huge hands. One of Pete's famously rich stews must have been bubbling in the back, as the entire saloon was filled with its rich aroma.

George shuffled up to the bar and sat down. Pete walked out of a prep area located behind the bar and greeted him.

"George, how is your day going?"

George's face told the story. George paused, but did not feel like talking about his morning. "It's been a while, Pete, how are things going with you?"

"Not too bad. Harvest season is nearly over. Always a busy time for me." Pete leaned in closer to George over the bar. "And it makes the banker happy. But they run me off my feet. It's like my mother used to say about family. Glad to see them come. Glad to see them go."

Pete and George both chuckled.

"I actually have a bit of business with you this morning Pete," George stated.

Pete looked at George.

"I have promised Claude that I will pay for his beer this poker Thursday."

"That's not a cheap promise." Pete raised his eyebrows.

"So I want to see how much is left on my tab."

Pete opened a large well-worn book from under the bar, and flipped through a couple of pages. "Well, you do have some left, enough for a good breakfast maybe, but certainly not a night of drinking. However, I have some business with you first."

"Okay," said George. "What do you need?"

"A leak has shown up in the corner room upstairs, it showed itself during our last thunderstorm."

George nodded. "Which side?"

"North corner."

"Makes sense," said George. "That's the side that faces most of the weather. I can take a look?" he offered.

"Did you want something to drink first? inquired Pete.

"You know me too well." George grinned. "A George Breakfast Special please."

"Coming right up!" Pete grabbed a glass from the shelves behind the bar, and placed a tea strainer on its top. He took a pull from one of the beer taps on the bar, half filling the glass. The screen removed the thicker elements of the local beer. He then filled the rest of the glass from a water pitcher and passed it to George. George raised his glass. "Cheers," he said and took a sip.

"Of course, if you do end up fixing the leak, we can top your tab up, more than enough even for a night of Claude's drinking."

"Sounds great," said George, and stood up. "Shall we take a look?"

Pete walked out from behind the bar. "Kathy?" he shouted towards the back. A slim woman with long black hair emerged from the prep area. Pete was the only one who called her Kathy, everyone else at the bar called her Kat. "Can you keep an eye on things while I take George upstairs to look at the leak?" Kathy nodded.

George and Pete both walked up the staircase at the back of the saloon that extended up to a balcony. It wrapped around two sides of the second floor, functioning both as a hallway for room access, and a great people-watching spot when the saloon got busy.

When they reached the top of the stairs, a door swung open with a thud and a blonde woman, wet hair still stuck to her head, thick robes covering her body, emerged. She looked embarrassed when she noticed there were two men at the top of the stairs.

"Hello Lacy," said George. Lacy looked relieved that it was George and Pete.

"Mornin' George." She scuttled through another door, closing it behind her.

George looked over the balcony and shouted "Kat!" Kat looked up at them. "If a tall slim man in a blue blazer comes in looking for me, can you let me know?" Kat nodded. George took a long pull from his beer, and Pete and George headed into the corner room.

About twenty minutes later, the two emerged from the room with George talking. "I don't think it's going to be a big fix, and I have something that should be in today or tomorrow that can probably help it last a bit longer this time."

"Thank you, George. Appreciated as usual."

As they descended the curving staircase, George looked around the room but could see no sign of the tall gentleman. He asked Pete for a bowl of his stew and sat down by the front entrance. A few spoonfuls into his stew, the saloon doors swung open.

"Mr. Sneed!" called George.

The tall gentleman walked over to George's table, pulled out a chair and sat down. He pulled a telegram out of his pocket and unfolded it neatly on the table. He further flattened it with his hands. He looked at George and gave him a toothy smile. George noticed that his eyes were not smiling however.

"I understand that you are the, uh..." Mr. Sneed paused.

"Gentleman who will be building my bank?" finished George.

"Quite frankly sir, we could have had this conversation much sooner if you had been clearer a little bit earlier," Mr. Sneed continued with his large smile.

George replied, "I tend to be a lot less cooperative when someone accuses me of theft. Bad habit I have." George glared back.

Mr. Sneed stayed rigid and upright, the smile remaining painted on his face. "I notice that you have provided an eight-week estimate for building the bank. I think you can do a lot better and have it ready for me quite a bit sooner." The smile remained.

George leaned back in his chair and took a big breath in through his nose, exhaling it slowly. "I had dinner with Mr. Chamberlain and his fine family a few weeks ago when he first mentioned this job to me."

Mr. Sneed's smile visibly faded at the mention of his boss.

"When I gave him this estimate, he didn't even try to haggle, he simply approved it. Do you know why that is?"

The smile faded further and Mr. Sneed's mouth tightened considerably.

"I have worked various jobs for Mr. Chamberlain over the last five or so years, the biggest one being head Carpenter at Shnell's Textiles. Mr. Chamberlain does not invest five figures in a property lightly, but my prior work on the hotel, the bank expansion, and his house meant that he had grown to trust me. And I did as I promised, finished building the factory on time and on budget. Something that is not easy to do these days."

Mr. Sneed looked like he did not know how to react.

"After dinner, we retired to his parlour, and both had some of the smoothest brandy I have ever tasted. We then shared a couple of fine cigars. And after a brandy or two more, Mr. Chamberlain started talking about you."

Mr. Sneed's mouth tightened so much the George thought briefly, *that looks like an asshole*. He quickly banished the thought from his head and continued.

"Mr. Chamberlain is very impressed with you. He says you always work hard, have amazing focus, and haven't made a single error in his books over the four years you have been hired. And, even more importantly, you are as straight as an arrow, completely honest in your work."

George paused and looked at Mr. Sneed. Mr. Sneed relaxed visibly.

"I respect tremendously an honest man who takes his work seriously and works hard." George continued. "Just like me. I feel we may have gotten off to a rough start, but think we can both respect each other as professionals and appreciate the skills we have to offer. The bank is going to be built properly, on time, on budget, and is going to take eight weeks."

George waited. Mr. Sneed looked uncomfortable for a moment, and then replied, "When can you start?"

George replied, "I am going to start at the beginning of next week. In the meantime there are a few shipments of supplies that are critical to getting it done on time, things such as hardware, metal bars for the teller windows, windows, doors, shingles and a Daisy floor safe. If these arrive on time, then there will be no problem meeting the schedule. Can you follow up on these deliveries to ensure they are delivered on time?"

Mr. Sneed replied, "If you give me complete shipping manifests and the names of the delivery companies, I can certainly take care of that for you."

This was the precise and efficient Mr. Sneed that George had expected. George stood up and held out his hand. Mr. Sneed did the same and they shook on it. "Nice doing business with you," stated George.

"And you," Mr. Sneed replied. He quickly and precisely walked out of the saloon.

George sat back down and started back into his now-lukewarm stew. When finished, he took a last long pull of his beer.

CHAPTER 9

GEORGE STEPPED OUT OF THE SALOON onto the new boardwalk and turned right to proceed up the street. His feet thunked on the new wooden surface, uneven with crude lumber just like the station. Two cowboys were having a smoke outside on the veranda of the saloon as George walked by. One gave George a brief nod; George nodded back.

George walked past the printing shop and spotted the owner hunched over the printing machine. George assumed he was working on the *Junction Herald*, the local paper.

George then paused in front of the Service Mercantile. Some robust-looking tools were carefully arranged in front of the shop: shovels, picks and brooms. A couple of barrels were on either side of the door; one was for garbage, the other was full of lemons for sale, with a "Fresh from the South Coast" sign on them. George looked at the carefully arranged merchandise through big windows at the store front, and pushed open the door to walk inside.

There, standing in front of neatly arranged shelves of tins and tools, jars of candy and spices, packages of tea and sugar, was Mr. Service. Arms folded, he wore a big smile on his face.

"Mr. Wainwright, it's been a while! Good to see you!" He opened his arms and George and Mr. Service shared a hearty, back-patting hug.

"I have been working in Yorktown for a bit; good to be back, definitely." George returned the smile. "The place is looking great."

"Why thank you. Yes, got 'the boy' to help out. Takes some convincing, had to tear him away from his books, but he is a good worker once started. What can I do for you today?"

"I believe I have a couple of things to pick up, and need some paper. Five sheets of twelve by twenty-four, if you have it."

"Of course." The shopkeeper reached under the counter and carefully pulled out five sheets of paper. "Your other items are in the back." Mr. Service started heading there.

"Actually..." George stated hesitantly. The shopkeeper paused.

George continued. "I can pay you for them today but won't be picking them up yet." The shopkeeper's shoulders drooped.

"Is that going to be an issue?" asked George.

"Come take a look.." Mr. Service motioned George to the back. They both walked through the door and George looked around. From floor to ceiling, it was packed with goods. So much so that the back door was not usable at the time. "I got a *lot* of inventory right now; I want to have as much as I can with the locals preparing for winter. Saves them a trip to Yorktown and I get the money too, which helps." He smiled. "And here are your, uh, rolls?" he said.

"And there they are!" George looked at the two tall black rolls taking up precious space at the side of the storage room.

"And what are they?" asked the shopkeeper.

"Those are two rolls of tar cloth." The shopkeeper nodded, and raised his eyebrows. George continued, "They are a roofing material, quick to apply, completely waterproof." Mr. Service looked skeptical. "You can use them as is, or put them under shingles as a bit of extra insurance against leaking. I am going to be using some on one corner of Sticky Pete's."

Mr. Service nodded. George continued, "And I can't pick them up today because Thunder is, uh, not wagon-pulling today."

"Oh," replied the shopkeeper, looking down.

"But, I tell you what, if the wagon is still out tomorrow, I will personally carry them home one at a time. You obviously need the space."

Mr. Service nodded and patted George on the back. "Much appreciated. Let's ring you up."

They walked to the front of the store again, and the shopkeeper started pushing large buttons on the till, making the dollar amounts pop up on little signs behind a glass window. "The paper is one cent a sheet." The 1 cent popped up five times with a rattle in the little window. "The *Herald* is also one cent." Another 1 cent popped up. "And the, uh, tar cloth is a dollar-sixty a roll." Now a $1, 50 cents and 10 cents popped up twice. "For a grand total of..." Mr. Service looked at the window in the cash register. A $3 sign was up along with 20 cents, 5 cents and 1 cent. A small bell rang inside the machine. "Three twenty-six. Will that be cash or tab?"

"Today, my fine friend, it will be cash." George reached into his pocket and pulled out the change JJ had given him a few days ago.

"Cash is always accepted," said Mr. Service. They completed the transaction.

"One more thing..." said George, suddenly remembering, "I am working on building the bank a couple of doors down for the next few weeks."

"I wondered if that was going to be you."

"And I need some short-term help, someone who has some skill with wood, and a basic labourer would be nice."

"Well, if I could be so bold as to suggest my son?" Mr. Service suggested. "He doesn't have much experience with wood yet, but he is a large fourteen-year-old boy, a man-child essentially. He listens well and works hard."

"Okay, can he start next Monday?"

"He sure can!"

"Well let him know to be at the site at eight a.m. Looking forward to working with him."

"Thank you sir!" Mr. Service waved as George exited the store, papers in hand.

George walked up the wagon trail to the cabin, not wanting to take the shorter trail through the woods for fear of wrecking the paper. Much to his surprise, as he arrived, he saw Maddie leading Thunder around the yard by the reigns, with the wagon in tow. He waved to Maddie enthusiastically. Maddie shook her head sternly. George took this to mean that this was not the time for a conversation, and instead went inside the cabin for some food and tea.

About twenty minutes later, Maddie came through the front door. "Thunder is still a bit tense, but doing way better."

"I can't believe he was pulling the wagon!" said George.

"I know! We were walking around, and, I think it might be because I didn't saddle him, he thought we were going to be pulling the wagon. So he walked right up and stood in front of it, ready to go! I took my time hooking up the tack, but there were no problems. We must have walked around for at least an hour or two before you got home. I have also let him go down by the river, where the fresh grass is. I think he likes that spot."

"Will he be ready for tomorrow?"

"I think so, but just me driving the wagon. He gets a little more tense when you're around. He needs time."

"Not a problem, if we can pick up the windows tomorrow and a couple of things from the Mercantile, that's all we need."

"I think that's reasonable. We can see how it goes." Maddie nodded thoughtfully.

"And... I have some work for you!" stated George.

"Oh, just what I need. Because I have so much free time." Maddie rolled her eyes.

"It's paid work, some of it," stated George.

"Well, okay then. What do you need?" Maddie replied with a bit more enthusiasm.

"Two things. The first is that I got the bank job set up, so I will need the bank sign painted on the facade above the windows in a few weeks, and also some window painting. If you can let me know exactly what supplies you need, I can pass that on to Mr. Sneed, our new banker, usual dark green bank colours."

"Okay," Maddie agreed.

"And also, I got some paper down at the Mercantile." George pointed to the table. I need some signs to post in a few places, using your amazing writing abilities, to promote my new buildings. Something like, I don't know..."

George made a grand gesture, "Cabin in a day! All the wood and supplies you need for a twelve by fourteen cabin, pre-cut and ready to use. Includes windows, doors, all needed hardware, roofing material and pre-cut wood. Most people can build it in a single day! Eighty dollars." George shrugged. "Of course, with your way with words, you can probably come up with something even better. Whatever you think will sell."

Maddie smiled. "I think I can come up with something; do you also have your plans ready to go?"

"I do, I will grab them from the barn. With the windows shipment and the roofing material from the Mercantile, and all the wood I pre-cut over the summer, I have enough for six cabins." George considered. "I hope we can sell at least a couple. That way I can work here more and not need to go to Yorktown."

Maddie nodded confidently. "I think they are a good idea, and I haven't seen anything else like it." She smiled. "You go grab your plans; I am going to get started right away while there is still a good light."

George left the cabin and headed out to the barn, his spirits considerably lifted after the start to the day.

CHAPTER 10

THE NEXT MORNING, George was up first. He went down the ladder to the back of the house, and then passed through to the front living area. He stoked the potbellied stove and grabbed the kettle to make tea. It was empty, and the metal bucket on the kitchen table was also empty.

He stepped out into the cool morning air and walked down the short path to Murray creek. He filled the bucket with the cold clean water, stood up, and took a moment to listen to the creek bubbling and rushing over the rocks. He felt good, like the day was full of promise.

He walked back to the cabin being careful not to spill any water from the bucket he filled just a bit too full. He opened the door quietly and filled the kettle with water, placing it on the stove. A quick toss of another piece of wood into the stove meant the water would be ready for tea just a bit sooner.

He looked over at the table and saw that Maddie had finished the posters. He had not seen them yet. Maddie had worked into the fading light of the day, and lamplight and other chores meant he had not thought to check. He walked over to the table and held up a sign.

George was impressed, Maddie's penmanship was clear and clean, just like it was on the many signs she had painted for the buildings in Junction. And he liked the way

WAINWRIGHT
Quick Buildings

If it's not Wainwright, it's not built right.

Cabins, storage, outbuildings.

Everything you need to build a new building within a day or two!

Includes:

–Clear instructions for a complete 168 square foot building.
–All wood needed pre-cut to length.
–Windows and doors pre-made and ready to go.
–All hardware including nails, bolts and hinges.

All this for only $80!

Contact George or Maddie Wainwright

she had taken his ideas and made them clear and sound positive. And on a deep level, he appreciated both the help and the belief in what he was doing.

The kettle started to boil. George also noted that she had finished a list of painting supplies to be passed along to Mr. Sneed. He then headed quietly to the back of the cabin and stood at the base of the ladder wondering if he should ask Maddie if she also wanted tea.

"Yes please," a quiet voice came down from the loft. She must have heard his steps coming to the back of the cabin.

George returned out front and made them both a cup of tea. Maddie joined him shortly.

"Very nice job on the posters!" exclaimed George, holding one up and appreciating it again.

"Glad you like it. I know you wanted to post it as a cabin, but I thought you might get more interest if it was a bit more... versatile."

George nodded, smiling. "And the Wainwright build right thing, very good."

Maddie smiled knowingly and sipped her tea.

A little while later they were both at the barn. Thunder had been fed and watered; Maddie was taking him over to the wagon. George had just finished cleaning out Thunder's stall. Maddie turned to George as he approached.

"I want to be the only one with Thunder and the wagon this morning; he is more relaxed with just me at the reigns."

"That's totally fine," said George. "I will grab the posters and head into town. We can meet at the train station and load up those windows."

Maddie agreed.

George headed down the trail towards the station, and looked around for Claude. Claude wasn't in the station, around the station, or anywhere he could see. He looked down the track to Yorktown and saw nothing. He walked to the other end of the station platform and looked west. Here he could see a small figure struggling with something heavy, the item that person was carrying would occasionally clank against the crushed-rock track base as it was being lugged. George put down his posters on the platform and put a rock on the top to stop them blowing away. He jogged up to Claude, who appeared to be struggling with the bottom half of a cast-iron pot potbellied stove.

Without saying a word, George grabbed the side of the stove opposite Claude and lifted it, heading down the track as well. Claude looked like he wanted to protest, but his red sweat-covered face thought better of it. They both carried it down the track until they arrived at the track switch that gave Junction its name. Claude put down the cast-iron component. George noticed there were some long, hollow, square pieces of iron also brought down the tracks.

"Switch heater" Claude said by way of explanation. "When we get a blizzard, I can light a coal fire in this thing, and it will keep the switch points ice free. Better than them freezing and having to dig them out and beat them with a sledgehammer."

"Makes sense."

Claude asked tensely, "No excuses for the windows today?"

George smiled, and pointed back at the station platform. Maddie was rounding the corner and lining the wagon up with the side of the platform. Neither man said a word as they headed back to the station.

After filling the wagon with windows, Maddie said, "I would rather leave this here and walk into town. Crossing the tracks would be hard on the windows." Maddie looked down at Claude who had been watching them load the windows. "And I am sure Claude won't mind the wagon here for a half hour or so?"

Claude's mouth opened a couple of times to say something, and thought better of it both times. He then stated in an official voice, "No train due for at least an hour; Thunder should be fine."

"Thanks Claude!" called out Maddie as she and George crossed the tracks on the short walk to town and the Mercantile.

"Where would I find your friend, Mr. Sneed?" asked Maddie as they started walking down Main Street.

"Good question. Not the bank, as I haven't built it yet!" George started laughing loudly but stopped quickly as Maddie wasn't.

"He might be staying at Sticky Pete's. Or if not, Pete would probably know where he is staying."

"Then I am going in here," said Maddie before heading up the steps and into the saloon. "Oh! Give me a poster," she said, holding out her hand. "We can probably post one here." George did so, and Maddie quickly turned and went inside the saloon. George walked into the Mercantile a few steps further.

Mr. Service was behind the counter weighing out two 2-pound bags of coffee. "Mr. Wainwright!"

"Mr. Service!" George replied. "I am here for the tar cloth and..."

"And...?" the shopkeeper replied after George paused.

George put one of the posters on the counter of the store. "I am wondering if there is somewhere you can display this for me."

Mr. Service looked it over with great interest. "I can post this, yes..." he said, trailing off.

At that moment, the door burst open, and a local farmer, Robert, strode in. Mr. Service was putting up the poster on the front of the counter.

"Did you see what George has asked me to post?" he asked Robert.

Robert took a few seconds to read it impatiently then said gruffly, "No one's going to want to buy one of your paper buildings, George!"

George was taken aback by this response. He was momentarily defensive, and felt like pointing out how his buildings made up almost half of the town of Junction, and that they had survived numerous blizzards including the blizzard of '78, but then he realized something.

Mr. Service exclaimed, "Not so fast there Robert, if George is building them, I am sure they are strong; in fact I am considering one myself." He looked meaningfully at George.

George looked at Robert. "What is up, Robert? You seem grumpy, even for you..."

Robert snorted at George. George replied, "Something *is* up. What is it?"

"Why don't you ask Brad!" Robert growled, and exited the store with a loud bang of the door.

George looked at Mr. Service. Mr. Service raised his eyebrows and shrugged his shoulders. "Well, I am serious about the building. It would solve my storage problem and... the price is right. Give me a chance to get together enough cash from my fall inventory and I can pay you. Are they ready to go?"

"They sure are."

"And what do I need to do?"

"Well, you will need level ground, about fourteen by sixteen feet. And make sure it drains well; wood shouldn't sit in a puddle. You can make the foundation out of four logs in a square if you like, or have a well-draining foundation made out of rock."

The shopkeeper replied, "This sounds like the perfect task for my boy." He grinned. "When he isn't helping you with the bank of course."

At that moment, Lorraine walked in through the front door. "He didn't even buy anything, did he?" referring to Robert. Both George and Mr. Service shook their head.

"Is something wrong?" asked George.

"It's Mort."

"Oh no!" said George.

"Nothing too serious, Robert noticed this morning that Mort's hooves looked a little chipped. So we decided to get some shoes for him. Normally he is just walking around our sections, but the ground is really hard this year with the dry summer. But when we got to Brad's, Brad would not shoe him."

"Why not?"

"He said Mort's hooves were too soft. Which doesn't make any sense. So we took Mort down to the livery and had the vet take a look, and the vet agreed. He said Mort should not do any more farm work for a while to prevent splitting, and let his hooves dry out. Which makes no sense because everything is so damn dry." Lorraine sighed and shrugged. "And Robert is pissed off because he is getting through the end of harvest; he has three or more days of bringing in the sheaves while the boys are threshing. He is worried that leaving them out in the field will cause problems. And if it rains. Then they could rot or get mold. So, yes... he is not a happy man today."

"Can't Spirit help out?" asked George.

"Oh, Spirit is a great horse," said Lorraine, "but she is not a workhorse. Not like Mort. Mort will just calmly plod all day pulling the heavy wagon with no issues. Spirit can only pull the light wagon. And after a full morning of work, she loses her steam. Starts to take more and more convincing to get her moving. She is basically not useful at all after a half day of hard pulling." Lorraine looked concerned.

Just then, Maddie walked in. She looked at the faces in the shop and asked, "What's going on?"

George replied. "Mort is out of commission for a while and they haven't finished harvest. And Spirit is not up to the task, so... they are worried they won't get the rest of the harvest in time."

Maddie thought for a moment. "Well, Thunder is doing remarkably well and could probably help out over the rest of the week. And you can also borrow the wagon. I mean, Thunder is no Mort, but he could certainly help double your pace of harvest from just Spirit. And George would be happy to help out, wouldn't you George?"

George's eyes widened. "Uh, yes? I mean, of course. Of course! I can head over tomorrow morning and we can get started."

"That is very generous of you," said Lorraine. "Give me a few moments to discuss with Robert. I am sure it will be fine." Lorraine left.

Mr. Service went into the back of the store.

Maddie said, "I have given the painting list to Mr. Sneed; he is staying at the printers, on the second floor of course."

"Of course, it would be cheaper and quieter than the saloon," replied George. Mr. Service came out of the back of the store with a roll of tar cloth on his shoulder.

"This is for you," he said to George and passed it to him.

"Put it on my back," said Maddie.

"You sure?" said George, "pretty heavy."

"I am strong. You forget," said Maddie grinning. Maddie leaned forward and George put it on her back. She bumped and shifted the weight to balance the roll, and held it underneath with both hands. She kicked open the door and headed out.

George turned and looked at Mr. Service. "Robust Scottish blood," he said.

"I'll say," replied Mr. Service. He got the second roll out of the back and gave it to George.

George noticed Mr. Service looking dubious. "If you are not comfortable with just the tar cloth on the roof, we can add shingles on top. I can get them for a wholesale price."

Mr. Service nodded. "Let me consider it. As is will be fine for now."

George heaved the tar cloth roll onto his shoulder and headed out, Mr. Service holding the door open for him.

"Thank you sir!"

"Thank *you* sir!"

George followed his rushing wife back to the station and wagon.

CHAPTER 11

GEORGE LET THUNDER ESTABLISH his own pace to the farm the next morning. The wagon wound down the cart trail to the main farmhouse and barn where Robert, Spirit, and a farm wagon were waiting for them.

Robert motioned to George to follow, and they both headed down to the far side of the north section of the farm. Dozens of sheaves of wheat stood in the field, ready to be picked up. Robert stopped his wagon at the front edge of the sheaves and got off. George stopped his wagon a few paces away and stepped off, following Robert.

Robert walked over to one of the sheaves and turned to George.

"They are more awkward than heavy," Robert said. "But you have to be careful. Too much jolting will knock the seed off, which is, really, the whole point." He picked up the wheat bundle and shifted it to his back. To George, it looked comical, because as he walked away, it looked like the wheat bundle had sprouted legs and was plodding through the field.

George walked up to Robert just as he got to his wagon.

"When you put it in the wagon, do it gently. And make sure the heads are not hanging over the edge; it will drop more seed."

That was the extent of the conversation that morning. both George and Robert loaded their wagons and brought their loads back to the barn for drop-off. At the other end of the barn, Robert's sons were thrashing the wheat. The barn was designed for this specific task, so it had two large doors opposite each other on the far end. As the wheat was thrashed, the prairie breeze blew through the doors, carrying wheat straw and dust from the thrashing process outside of the barn.

Even though he was warm from the heat, George did up the top button on his shirt. Tiny pieces of wheat would trickle down his back, stick to his sweat, and cause powerful itching. He took off his shirt momentarily, brushed off his back best he could, and put the shirt back on, done all the way up. George did not mind the work; it was tiring but not difficult. And being out in the sun, the sound of the horses, and the quiet company of someone else working was satisfying.

After about four hours of steady work, George could see Spirit was getting tired. Robert shouted out a lot more "HEEEYAA's!" to get her moving, and her movement was slow and plodding, her back was arched and she held her head low when stopped. After a couple of trips with Robert that required a lot of encouragement, Robert turned to George when he arrived at the barn with his latest load.

"After this load," Robert said, "Sweep out your cart and shovel it into the screen over there." He pointed to a large wooden box with a wire screen on the top. "We can save any seed that is dropped in the wagon that way." Robert did the same and, after completion turned to George and announced, "Lunch."

George followed Robert to the farmhouse. They sat down outside on some logs around a firepit with Robert's boys. Lorraine came out of the house with a big plate of bread cut into chunks, and a plate of smoked and spiced beef cut the same way. She then headed back into the house and brought out lemonade for each of them in jars, and passed them around.

"Nothing like lemonade on a hot day!" she proclaimed.

George sipped the lemonade and said gratefully, "This has to be just about the best damn lemonade I have ever tasted!"

The boys laughed and Robert grunted in approval, raising his jar slightly before gulping down the rest of it. While Robert and George did not speak, the boys were talking animatedly about the latest steam tractors they had seen in Yorktown.

"Did you see the big one, they said it's thirty horsepower! Thirty horses! They said it can plow a section in a week. A whole section!" said one boy.

Another replied, "And, most of 'em come with a belt drive, so you can run other machines off of it, like a threshing machine," moving his eyebrows up and down for emphasis.

"And," said a third boy, "you wouldn't have to worry about soft hooves getting in the way of work."

Robert snapped, "Enough, gabber—back to work boys, now!" His sons quickly stood up and slunk back over to the barn.

Robert and George finished another couple of hours of work, until Spirit had had enough. George watched as Robert "HEEEYAA-ed" his way back to the barn, and he decided that Thunder could handle another couple of trips before finishing his day.

He was just sweeping out the cart to finish up when Lorraine approached. "You stayin' for dinner?" she asked. "You are welcome to."

George replied, "Not today. Maddie is cooking up some fish. But ask me again tomorrow."

Lorraine said, "Suit yourself," and walked away. George finished up and headed home.

The next day went pretty much the same way, two men working the fields quietly with horses and carts. Robert's sons worked in the barn. Lunch was considerably quieter though; the boys had learned that silence could extend the lunch a few minutes more.

Just as the sun was going down for the evening, Robert and George brought in the last load of sheaves. Spirit was not pleased at all with the longer day, and Robert led her by the reigns rather than riding the wagon for the last few loads. They emptied out the carts and Robert stood at the barn door looking back over the fields. He took a deep breath.

"Feels good, gettin' a job done," he said. George nodded in agreement. Robert looked towards the front of the barn where he could still hear the boys threshing. He motioned to George to follow him. They walked around the side of the barn, and Robert took a long hard look at the farmhouse. Much to George's surprise, he pulled on the side of the barn and opened a narrow door that would go undetected if one didn't know it was there.

"Hurry," said Robert, and they both darted inside. Robert closed the door and waited a moment as both of their eyes adjusted to the dim light. George looked around after a couple of minutes and saw a large copper kettle, some copper pipe wound in coils, and noted the distinct smell of charcoal.

Robert smiled and pulled out two jars, placing them under a spigot on the side of the kettle. "I already removed the head and have tested this." He paused. "And its good." He passed one of the jars of clear fluid to George and hoisted his in the air. "Cheers," he said, swallowing his in one gulp. Robert shuddered slightly, and a broad smile widened on his face. "Will put hair on your chest."

George lifted his jar, and took a big gulp of the fluid. It was like drinking liquid fire. He felt all of the hair on his body stand on end, crackles went down his spine, and it took a great deal of effort not to throw up on the spot. His body then started shaking and he started coughing.

Robert laughed heartily, then said, "Shhhhh, shhhhhhhh. Quiet." He chuckled again. He pulled a glass flask from his pocket and placed it under the spigot, filling it. "For you," he said, passing it to George. George took the flask and nodded in thanks, putting it in his pocket.

They snuck out of the barn both feeling considerably improved, satisfaction from hard work and the moonshine both providing a warm glow.

George and Robert walked over to the house and sat on the logs located in the back. Robert's boys came over. "Light the fire boys, and then leave us be." The boys obediently did as they were told and headed back to the farmhouse.

"It's good to have sons," said Robert. "Useful when they stop complaining." Both men laughed.

George, hesitant to bring it up but curious, asked about Mort. "Ahhh, Mort," sighed Robert. "He is doing great; I think he will be up and at 'em next week. You know..." said Robert, leaning towards George. "One of Mort's favourite places to stand is at the far side of the east section, down by Murray Creek. I think he likes watching the local wildlife, the cows in the next section, and the quiet at that end of the section."

"There is a watering trough down there that straddles the fence. That way, it's shared between the two sections; the cows and horses can both use it." George nodded in understanding.

"Well, about five years ago we installed a windmill pump down there, to take water from the creek and fill the trough. It was a pain in the you-know-what to fill that thing every day— short walk to the creek, but long walk down the section. It works well, so well in fact, that we don't go down and check it that much, it just... takes care of itself."

Robert took another deep sigh and leaned back. Taking another quick sip of his flask, he said. "Well, maybe a little too good. Turns out, the trough down there had rusted through the bottom, and was leaking water out where it was flowing back to the creek. Made a big muddy mess that, Mort, not bein' so bright, stood in when he was gazing over the fence. So, another fixing job to add to the list, and now we know why his hooves were soft."

George nodded and smiled. He took a quick pull on his flask and two quick coughs blasted out before he caught himself. Robert asked "Have you seen these steam tractors, George?"

George nodded. "They are impressive, noisy machines; you think they are any use?"

Robert shrugged. "Well, the first problem is money. Coming up with that kind of money is not easy. Even paying all those labourers after harvest is less than one quarter of that. But I also worry. I have heard lots of stories about how dangerous they are; all those belts and gears can grab clothing, and within seconds, well, you ain't farming anymore. And, the damn things can also blow up."

George nodded. Robert looked thoughtful and stated, "And I worry about the boys and farming. Farming is all about getting to know the land. The seasons, what a dry spring means, what a wet spring means. I can pick up a clod of soil, squeeze it, and know if it's good farmland,

and what will grow well on it. That's why we chose these four sections. Rich soil, Murray creek at the bottom, the hardwood forest on the other side. It seems like all these shortcuts might lead to something that is not... quite... farming." Robert shrugged.

"I understand," said George, and continued, "and from what I have heard, you cannot use them when it's wet out; they sink and get stuck. And what the hell can pull one of those out!" Robert laughed and, with a quick glance around, they both pulled out their flasks and clinked them together.

"Cheers!"

George felt as if his stomach was going to burst. A fine farm harvest dinner with roast beef, potatoes, turnips, and rich farm gravy filled every corner of his stomach. He looked at the remains of the feast before him, and marvelled at the amount of food the farm boys could put away. One of the boys leaned back in his chair and blasted a short burp across the table.

"Boys," came the warning from the kitchen.

Another boy leaned forward and let go a five-second-long belch then leaned back with satisfaction.

Robert then leaned back in his chair and let such a blast forth that the air shook and it felt like someone had fired off a shotgun—you could feel the blast in your chest.

His sons nodded, impressed, while Dolly wrinkled her face in disgust.

George, not wanting to be left out of this rite of harvest passage, leaned back and pushed out what he assumed was going to be a mighty expulsion of post-dinner air. Instead, something went wrong and it blasted out of his nose. First with a high squealing sound, then a massive double snort.

The entire table erupted into laughter, one of the boys laughing so hard that tears came out of his eyes.

"What the hell was that?" exclaimed Lorraine as she came out of the kitchen. The boys weakly pointed to George, still laughing. "I have never heard such a noise as that come out of a person before!" exclaimed Lorraine.

After the table calmed down, George stood up and politely excused himself. "Thank you very much, madam, a real feast, so appreciated."

Lorraine replied, "No problem George, you know you and Maddie are always welcome here."

George walked to the door, and was just about to leave when Robert tapped him on the shoulder.

"Poker?" Robert asked.

"See you at Pete's," replied George and headed out into the evening.

CHAPTER 12

GEORGE HEARD THE GUITAR MUSIC and active sounds of a busy night before he even got to the door of Sticky Pete's. As he stepped inside, he made careful note of the three poker tables to ensure he would get a seat. The high-roller and middle table were nearly full, but the small-stakes table he normally played at still had seats.

He walked over to the bar and waited for a few moments as Kat poured beer and whisky for the various bar patrons. She saw George and simply said, "Usual?" George nodded in response. Kat grabbed a beer pre-poured and pre-prepared to George's specifications under the bar, and passed him a tin marked GW. He took a sip of the beer, and poured the change out of the tin into his hand. The tin was his bankroll, money he just used for playing poker. "Has Pete made you aware of the arrangement with Claude?" Kat nodded.

He walked over to the poker table and greeted his friends. "Mr. Service... Pete, I see you are taking a break and playing tonight." Pete nodded and smiled. "JJ, did not expect to see you here!"

JJ shrugged. "Always happy to take your money," he joked.

George saw another face he recognized. "Farm Boy!" Even at twenty, Farm Boy looked very young compared to the regulars, and a bit uncomfortable, but smiled. Then Claude rushed in and sat down at the table. He glared at George. "My beer?"

George said, "I know. I have told Kat." Claude remained seated and continued glaring. "Well go get your beer; I ain't also your barkeep!" barked George. Claude got up and went over to the bar.

He got his first beer and said, "Keep this glass full," to Kat.

The chairs at the table were filling up fast, except for one very large one at the end. A new person, with dark black hair and crooked teeth sat in the big chair. "I wouldn't sit there," advised Mr. Service. The man looked annoyed.

"I don't see no reservation sign," he said.

"That chair is Brad's," said Mr. Service.

"Well, Brad will have to sit in one of the other chairs then, won't he." The man crossed his arms.

George noticed that the saloon had gone quiet, except for the guitar player playing "My Bonnie," and he followed the gaze of most of the patrons. There, walking down the stairs with a confident, unhurried, swinging gait was a woman with blonde hair high above her head in curls; fancy black dress with white frills on the neck, sleeves, and around the hem; and a plunging neckline. She walked through the bar patrons ignoring wolf whistles and dexterously slapping away any hands that got too curious. She sat down at George's table, looked at each of the men and winked. "Well boys, I am going to get your money one way or the other."

Farm Boy, who was by chance sitting right beside her, turned beet red. At that moment another figure of note appeared in the door of the saloon. At three hundred fifty pounds, Brad nearly filled the door, and many heads turned as he paused to look around. He then started over towards the poker tables. "That's Brad," whispered Mr. Service to the new table patron, who hastily moved to another seat at the table without a word. Most of the table patrons chuckled. The new player scowled in his seat.

"Well boys," said Brad in a booming voice, rubbing his hands together. "Let's play some poker!" He sat down in the only chair that would fit him.

Animated conversation between the players ensued. The new player looked confused, and turned to George. "Are we gonna play some poker soon or what?" George replied, "A couple more minutes and the dealers will come out." George looked at the new player. "My name's George." The new player said nothing.

Lacy spoke. "That's the part where you say your name, honey." His eyes grew wide and he stammered out, "Mike." Lacy replied, "Well pleased to meet you, Mike," and held out her white-gloved hand like she expected a polite kiss. Mike took it and shook it awkwardly. Lacy laughed.

Three well-dressed dealers emerged from a back room and proceeded to the tables. The dealer for George's table sat down and put down a tray full of change. He stated, "As most of you know, this is the one-and-ten table, one-cent ante, ten-cent maximum bet or raise. Five-card stud, two draws of two and..." he paused for emphasis, "*no* wild cards. Ever. Now who needs some change?" Various players reached into their pockets and gave the dealer quarters and the occasional dollar, which the dealer exchanged for pennies, nickels and dimes.

The saloon doors swung wildly open and one of the sheriff's deputies rushed in and sat down on the last chair at George's table. "Sorry!" he said, out of breath. He looked at the dealer. "Deal me in!" All players put their one-cent ante in the middle, and the dealer shuffled the cards and dealt five to each.

"Full table tonight," remarked the deputy. A couple of players agreed, and George smiled at the promise of lots of action.

As George usually did, he played fairly tight over the first hour, only playing his cards and betting when he had very good cards. Otherwise, he enjoyed the beer, the conversation, the music, and observing other players to determine betting habits and tells, the way they showed on their faces and bodies a bluff or a good hand.

The dealer called first break after an hour. George headed out to the veranda outside. JJ and a few others were outside as well. JJ called George over. "I noticed your sign at the Mercantile," he said. "You still have some of those buildings left?" George responded, "Sure do." Pete sat beside the two of them and started to smoke. George introduced JJ.

"JJ was just expressing some interest in one of my pre-made buildings," said George to Pete.

Pete said to JJ, "It's probably pretty good if George made it; he built this place, bit by bit over the years, with some help of course."

JJ turned to George. "In that case, I probably want to pick one up, while I am pulling in some decent money. The canvas is beginning to rot at the bottom, and when I attempt to repair it, its brittle and doesn't hold thread. I was going to have to replace it anyway. Will you deliver?"

"Oh definitely. I can even help build it if you like; I know where you live." JJ held out his hand. They shook on it.

"Poker!" a voice called from the door. They all headed inside for the next hour.

The second hour started, and the beer and other spirits were having an effect, with players betting a lot more and showing their emotions much more on their faces. George took full advantage and ended up with three more dollars than he had started the hour with, a very good return on the low-stakes table. He was surprised to see Mr. Sneed join the high-roller table, *didn't seem like the gambling social type,* thought George.

After a second break, the third hour was even more raucous. Claude was having an incredible run of luck, with full houses, flushes and straights hitting routinely. His good luck and unlimited alcohol put him in a tremendous mood, with him sometimes singing out his responses and standing and dancing when he hit yet another big hand. Lacy made careful note of his stack of money building up in front of him. Mike was not having such luck and kept reaching into his pocket to get more cash for change to keep playing.

George was the butt of the usual jokes at the expense of his hunting prowess, but he was used to it so it didn't phase him. At one point someone said, "He doesn't even own a rifle!"

"Or a sidearm," George said, shrugging it off.

Farm Boy was loosening up socially but was staying tight with his cards. A hand finished with just him and Lacy playing against each other as everyone else had folded their hands. They raised and re-raised each other until there was a dollar in the pot, a good-size. "What do you have, Farm Boy?" asked Lacy, "A pair of aces?" Farm Boy shook his head no, and laid down his cards to show them. "Two pair, kings and 4's." "Crap," said Lacy, "I only have a pair of queens. Take the pot..." she said.

Farm Boy flashed Lacy a huge smile and scooped up his winnings.

After the final hour, the dealer stood up and thanked everyone for coming. A few of the players, including George and Pete, tipped the dealer with some dimes. A couple of the players howled in protest, especially Claude. However, with some grumbling and mostly good spiritedness, the majority of players stood up and left the table. Lacy got up and walked over to Claude who was putting his ample stack of winnings in his pocket. She gave his shoulders a brief massage. "You want a nightcap after a great night honey?" she asked. Claude gave a big smile, stood up from his chair, turned and fell flat on his face. And didn't move. Brad picked him up by his arms and propped him up in a chair, where he immediately fell asleep. "That would be a no," stated Lacy.

She looked back at the table and noticed Farm Boy's stack of money that he was hastily putting into his pocket. She walked up to him and said, "You're going to buy me a drink." Farm Boy grinned, and they both headed over to the bar.

This left George, Mr. Service and Mike at the table. Mike was still complaining about the table shutting down. "Come on," he appealed desperately, "give me a chance to win some of it back. My luck is turning, I know it is."

George calmly said, "The dealer has left, Mike, time to pack it up for tonight," knowing full well that it *was* time for Mike to call it a night.

Mr. Service said helpfully, "I can deal a hand or two." Mike jumped at the chance, and threw in a penny ante. George sighed, "One more hand, then I have to get going." He threw in a penny and the hand was started. After they had their cards dealt, Mike bet out the maximum, ten cents, and George called it. After the first draw, Mike bet out the maximum and George called it. After the second draw, Mike bet out the maximum and George thought for a moment.

After the cards were first dealt, Mike looked happy. *That would mean he has a couple of decent cards,* George thought. But he put in two cards for a draw (replacement) and kept three, so George knew he had two or three good cards. After that draw, Mike again looked pleased, so George thought his hand had improved, but Mike also handed in two of his cards for the second draw, meaning only three of his five cards were good. And after the second draw, Mike looked again pleased with his cards, but not totally confident. George thought for a while and guessed Mike had a good two pair. George however had 3 threes, a hand that beat two pair.

So when Mike bet out the max bet at the end of the hand, George raised it. Mike instantly raised his raise, both at the maximum value. This went back and forth until all of Mike's money, just over a dollar, had been bet.

George called the final bet. Mike triumphantly laid his cards on the table and called out, "Two Pair, QUEENS and ACES!" He smiled broadly.

George said, "That is a good hand indeed my friend, but I am afraid I have 3 threes, which beats your hand." George laid the cards on the table.

Mike looked like he was going to explode. His eyes bulged out and a vein on his head and neck pulsed with his heart rate. "I AM NO FRIEND OF YOURS!" he shouted, and slowly stood up, giving George a hard stare.

For a moment it looked like he might punch George, but Mr. Service said, "Easy, Mike." Mike became aware of his surroundings and the many people now paying attention to what was happening. Furious, he turned and stormed out of the back of the bar.

George picked up his winnings from the night and took them over to the bar. Kat grabbed his tin can for the bankroll from under the bar and he dropped the change in. He said, "Take five bucks out of that, put four towards my tab and take one for yourself." Kat thanked George.

"Wow, good night!" said Mr. Service to George. George smiled weakly, but that last interaction had shook him. Mr. Service left the bar.

He looked at Claude, still asleep in his chair. George turned to Pete, now behind the bar. "Pete, can you help me get Claude on my back; I am going to take him to the station." George leaned forward and Pete heaved Claude onto his back. The combination of Claude's smaller size and George's carpentry-strengthened body meant this task wasn't too onerous. Pete held the swinging doors of the saloon open and George walked out into the night.

CHAPTER 13

GEORGE TRUDGED UP THE STAIRS at the far end of the station platform, walked towards the station door, stumbling twice on the uneven surface, nearly dropping Claude. Once he got to the door, he allowed Claude to slide down his back and flop onto the station platform. He reached into Claude's pockets, fumbling around his winnings of the night to find the station key. After some sighing and struggling, he found the key and opened the station door. He dragged Claude through the main station to a small room in the back. With some effort, he placed Claude on a cot located there and turned him on his side.

George noticed the gaps in the station walls were letting in small cold drafts, and he placed a couple of blankets over Claude. Claude shifted slightly and slept.

George locked the station door, slid the key under the door, and headed towards home. If the moon had been more than a sliver, he may have walked the shorter route through the poplar grove and known he was being followed. If his mind wasn't buzzing with beer and the night, he might have noticed footfalls in the grass twenty or so paces behind him. But he didn't, and instead got to his cabin weary and ready for sleep. He locked the cabin door and sat in the main room waiting for his mind to settle.

Suddenly the cabin door crashed open, wood splinters from the frame scattering away from the door lock. A dark figure appeared in the door, holding a five-shot revolver in its right hand. The figure laughed, and walked in through the door.

Mike was smiling, a predatory grin with crooked yellow teeth from ear to ear. "Well you arrogant piece of shit. You 'I don't have any guns' piece of crap. It's time to pay up!"

George felt a familiar and terrifying sensation course through his body. His mind remained clear, but both this body and voice were frozen. He could not move.

Mike sauntered through the living area. "You think you're so fucking smart. You and your friends laughing at me *all night*. Buying each other beers, clapping each others' backs, taking all of my money. TAKING. ALL. MY. MONEY!"

Mike stood in front of George and slowly raised his revolver to point it at him. "Well, I want my money *back*..." Mike smiled a smile that looked more like a grimace. "MY FRIEND."

George stayed frozen, his mind attempting to stay grounded. Thoughts and retorts raced through his head, but no actions, no words would come out.

"Well, now I am going to get my money, and maybe a bit more to sweeten the pot. Tell me George," Mike said leaning in close, "who has the better hand *now*? Mr. 'I Don't Hunt.'

Mr. 'So Fucking Smart.' Huh?" Mike looked at unmoving George.

"You just going to stay there, and not say anything? That's because you're too STUPID to speak, GEORGE; you know you're BEAT, and there's nothing you can do about it!"

Mike leaned in towards George again and awkwardly checked his pockets for money.

George thought, *Mike is off balance right now, if I could just grab that gun and his hand, I could probably surprise and overwhelm him.* George's body did not follow his commands; it did not move.

Mike's smile faded when he realized George's pockets were empty, and he stepped back a couple of paces. "WHERE IS THE FUCKING MONEY GEORGE? I *know* you have it, I saw the stack in front of you. WHERE is the FUCKING MONEY?

"You think you're so smart, well you ain't! I'll tell you what George, I'll make this real easy for you; you are going to tell me where the money is or..."

Mike pulled back the hammer on his revolver and pointed it straight at George's head. "Or, you're going to have a new hole in your head! WHERE IS THE FUCKING MONEY?"

At that moment a blast rang out from the back of the cabin, and both George and Mike watched in shock as Mike's hand and gun disappeared in a flash of smoke and shot.

The gun clattered into the corner of the cabin and went off, its bullet embedding harmlessly in a log by the cabin floor.

Mike screamed and staggered backwards, blood pouring like syrup out of what was left of his wrist. He backed into the cabin wall and slowly slid down into a sitting position, holding his wrist tight to stem the blood while grimacing and howling from the pain.

Maddie stepped into the front of the cabin, pointed the shotgun at Mike's head, pulled back the second hammer and put her finger on the second trigger. "I wouldn't do anything stupid," she stated calmly. She glanced at George before returning her iron gaze to Mike.

"Friend of yours?" she asked George.

George flopped down from his seat to the ground. His body felt thick and loose. He at first struggled to move at all, but then slowly stood on wobbly and heavy limbs. He awkwardly and with great effort staggered his way over to the gun on the floor, picking it up. The grip had been shattered and its structure warped. He studied the gun carefully for a moment before opening the cartridge and shakily pulling out the live bullets. He placed them in his pocket, throwing the gun into the kitchen bucket with a clang.

He looked at Mike, white faced, shaking on the floor and saying repeatedly, "My hand! My hand. My hand!"

George stammered at Mike, "You need to get your arm above your heart to slow down the bleeding." Mike did nothing. George shakily spoke out again slightly louder. "Get your arm in the air to slow the bleeding, Mike!" Mike did nothing.

Pointing the shotgun threateningly at Mike, Maddie screamed, "HANDS UP!" Mike immediately raised his arms in the air.

George left the front room and headed towards the pantry. Maddie heard the sound of shuffling and clinking glass. "What the hell are you doing, George! Getting a snack?!"

George emerged from the back area with a small brown glass bottle. He grabbed a spoon and opened the bottle. Carefully, regaining his steadiness, he poured a spoonful of laudanum and carried it over to Mike, who's gaze was still fixated on Maddie. Maddie yelled, "OPEN YOUR MOUTH!" Mike opened his mouth immediately and was surprised by a quick mouthful of laudanum. He reflexively swallowed it and looked confused at George.

"That's going to kill the pain a bit," George stated. He undid his belt buckle, and pulled his belt out of his pants. George grabbed a knife from the kitchen area, cut off the buckle and stood over Mike.

Maddie held the shotgun threateningly a couple of feet from Mike's head. "Don't fucking MOVE!"

George wrapped the belt leather a couple of times around Mike's forearm and pulled it tight, shuddering slightly at the sensation of bones grinding. Mike howled but his gaze did not move from Maddie. He wrapped the area a couple more times and then tightly knotted the belt. He cut the loose ends off, leaving Mike's arm securely wrapped. The bleeding slowed almost immediately.

"Can you get the horse ready while I watch this guy? Mike here is going to take a trip to the sheriff," George asked Maddie.

Maddie assessed George's wobbly legs and still stuttery voice and said, "I will watch this guy; you go get the horse ready."

George hesitated a moment, looked at Maddie's determined face and unwavering shotgun, and headed out of the cabin.

Maddie looked at Mike. Her mouth opened slightly a couple of times. She contemplated for a moment, and thought, *Why am I keeping my mouth shut right now?*

"You GODDAMN piece of SHIT! You festering ASSHOLE! Who the HELL do you think you are bursting into our cabin in the GODDAMN middle of the night! Waking me up so hard I nearly fell out of bed. Do you know how hard it is for me to sleep, MIKE?! Do you know how hard it is for me to sleep?"

Mike shook his head.

"No, you GODDAMN don't!" screamed Maddie. "You come into our house and point a gun at MY HUSBAND! Why? Because you can't take your goddamn losses like a man, that's why. What, did you lose a couple of bucks, maybe even 5 bucks! Well, boohoo, so sorry for you. BOO FRICKIN' HOO FOR YOU!"

"You know Mike, we first came to this country on a *goddamn* metal deathtrap of a boat ten or so years ago. And *George*, in his infinite wisdom, LOST OUR WHOLE GODDAMN SAVINGS in a poker game on that boat. One hundred dollars! EVERYTHING WE HAD. Did he whine about it?

No! Did he blame anyone else and try and shoot up the place? No! We had to eat crappy soda biscuits and rely on the charity of others for *two months* on that metal rusty stink barn! And he never once whined about losing! I didn't hold back on the other hand, if you can imagine that, Mike."

Mike didn't move, still looking at the shotgun.

"You keep looking at the shotgun," said Maddie, "I've seen what it can do to a face, and it ain't pretty."

Maddie paused for a moment, and sat down on the bench, wondering momentarily where George was but not moving the shotgun even slightly from its target.

"You know, Mike, you are a lucky man. You might not think it right now looking at your grunky arm, but you are."

Mike was looking at both his arm and the floor in front of him.

"PAY ATTENTION MIKE!" screamed Maddie. Mike obediently looked at Maddie once again.

She calmly continued. "A couple of years ago, I was sitting in this exact place. And I heard a scratching and glass breaking coming from the pantry. I thought the raccoons were back at it again, so I grabbed our shotgun and ran back to the pantry. I opened the door and saw instead it was a GODDAMN WOLVERINE! It had dug under our house and into the pantry. I shot at it but didn't get a clean shot, I think I hit its shoulder or hindquarters somehow. Luckily my apple spice preserve is slippery stuff, so when it lunged at me it slipped, and I managed to close the pantry door. He banged against it and reached his claws under it, bending the wood so much I thought he would break the door. Have you ever seen Wolverine claws, Mike?"

Mike shook his head.

"They are HUGE. I ran out of the cabin and to the barn, and reloaded the shotgun. I waited a while and went back into the cabin, but he was long gone. Probably back through the hole he dug in the floor."

Maddie breathed in. "So, the next day, George went to Yorktown and picked up a Remington Whitmore side by side shotgun. He took it to the blacksmith and got the barrel cut down to eighteen inches, so basically, at close range, what you shoot at is what you hit. You know why that makes you a lucky man Mike?"

Mike shook his head. Maddie explained "Because a side-by-side has two shots. If I'd only had one shot, I would have put it straight through your head. But I had two shots, one to get rid of your gun, and one to take care of you if that didn't work out. You see now, Mike? You see why you are lucky? You should thank that Wolverine for saving your life!" Maddie paused.

"Thank you, Wolverine," said Mike weakly.

Maddie smiled.

George opened the door to the cabin, carrying a coil of rope. Maddie did not move.

To both Mike and Maddie's surprise, George grabbed Mike by his feet and pulled him onto the living area carpet, Mike's head bonking on the floor. He pulled Mike further until his head was just protruding from the edge of the carpet.

"Arms by your sides Mike!" shouted George. Mike obeyed.

George grabbed one side of the carpet and rolled it over Mike, tucking it under his body. He then rolled Mike's body until he was neatly wrapped in a carpet tube. Maddie asked, "What on earth are you doing, George?"

George started wrapping the carpet with the rope, and turned to Maddie. "Ever try and take a man on a horse who doesn't want to ride?" Maddie understood and watched as George finished wrapping the rope around the carpet and securing Mike. Mike could not move.

Maddie, with some apprehension, released the hammer on the shotgun, and they both hauled Mike outside. With some straining they heaved Mike onto the horse, and securely lashed him to Thunder with leather straps. George climbed on the horse and gave a quick heel tap. Thunder and George headed in the direction of Junction.

CHAPTER 14

A FEW STEPS INTO THEIR JOURNEY, Mike started singing:

"By Blobby blibes oba de oblen. By Blobby blibes obla da blee..."

George recognized the laudanum and alcohol version of "My Bonnie" and grinned briefly. Instead of the usual track into town, George took a longer route that avoided Main Street. He did not want the curiosity or questions that might surround having a singing carpet roll with a head protruding. He took the alley behind the main buildings to reach the back door of the Sheriff's Office.

He passed the blacksmith just as the rear door opened. A tall, upright slim figure was outlined by the light inside; it quickly retreated and slammed the door shut. George thought, *That person wanted to be seen even less than I did.*

He pulled up at the back of the Sheriff's Office and tied Thunder off to the railing behind the building. He knocked on the door. No answer. He knocked louder and waited. He heard some shuffling inside, then a voice called out, "Yep!" A moment later, a disheveled sheriff opened the door.

"George!" he said. "Poker dispute at the bar?"

"No," said George. "I have a package for you." He pointed at the back of the horse.

"First for everything," the sheriff said, before walking up to the back of the horse. He leaned over and turned his head so that he could see Mike better.

"What's this guy's problem?"

"That's Mike," said George. "Help me get him down."

The sheriff and George untied the carpet roll from the back of the horse and brought it inside. In the light, Mike's face could be seen more clearly—his scraggly black hair, thick black beard, and crooked yellow teeth. "I think this might be a wanted man," said the sheriff. They put him in the jail cell in the office and the sheriff leafed through some papers on the desk.

"Yep, here it is. His name is Mike Drudge; he is wanted for theft." He took a look at the small print on the wanted poster. "Taking some stuff from hotel rooms, other small-time thefts, except for the hotel job, looks like. There's a fifty-dollar reward on this one." He pulled out another piece of paper from the desk and put it beside the reward poster. "Did he steal something from you?" George shook his head. "Let's get him out of your carpet."

They both untied the ropes holding the roll together, George pulled out the carpet while the sheriff steadied Mike. When Mike's arm was revealed, the sheriff swore. "Jesus Christ, that looks nasty. How did that happen?"

George paused. "Shotgun accident." The sheriff looked dubious. George continued. "It's like you always say, booze and guns don't mix."

The sheriff nodded suspiciously, "True enough, they don't." He thought for a moment. "I need to get the doctor for this. And of *course* the doctor is not at his office at this time of night; he is a twenty-minute ride out of town to his cabin. George, I am going to grab a deputy to watch this guy, and then head out to Doc. Can you watch him for a few minutes while I go? And fill out that sheet of paper I just got out describing how you picked this guy up. Then I can get you that reward."

"Of course," said George, "Of course."

The sheriff locked the cell door and hung the key on the wall. He put on his coat. "Thanks," he said and headed outside.

George sat down at the desk and looked at the wanted poster for Mike. It was all for theft, the biggest being the hotel robbery. Since the value was over one hundred dollars, he knew Mike was going to jail. George looked at Mike. Mike let out a low moan and clutched at his hand. George sighed. He remembered the look on Mike's face during the last poker hand. He remembered Mike's desperation at his cabin.

"Mike!" he called out. No response. "MIKE!" he shouted. No response.

He looked at the key on the wall.

Quickly, and with resolve, George grabbed the key and with haste opened the cell door and kneeled in front of Mike. "Mike!" he said, loudly and intensely. Mike opened his glassy, watery eyes.

"Listen, Mike! This is important!" Mike looked at George.

"I just told the sheriff you had a shotgun accident. Okay? You hear me? A shotgun accident!" George couldn't tell if Mike heard or not. Mike closed his eyes. George quickly stood up, locked the cell behind him, and sat back at the desk. He opened the inkpot for the quill the sheriff had left, and wrote on the reward piece of paper:

Give to church.

A few minutes later, the door rattled open and the deputy walked in. He nodded at George and looked in the jail cell. "Oh, nasty!" He paused. "So this must be Mike Drudge." He called out, "Mike!" Mike said nothing.

The deputy looked at the desk and picked up the paper George had written on. He looked at it for what seemed a long while, then turned to George with, "You sure? Fifty bucks is at least a week's work for most of us." George nodded. "Okay..." said the deputy with a wave.

George headed back out to Thunder, gave the horse a couple of neck rubs, and breathed in the calm of the night. He climbed onto Thunder and headed home.

When George arrived at the cabin, he exhaled in relief. The cabin was well lit and he could hear movement inside.

He allowed the routine of taking off Thunder's saddle and settling him down for the night to further calm his nerves before heading in.

Once inside, he saw Maddie on the floor with a scrub brush cleaning up the last of the blood. Maddie looked at George and explained, "I didn't like the idea of coming down to this, and I really don't like the idea of sleeping with it in my house." She brushed one area a couple more times then rubbed it with a towel.

She stood up. "We just got that rug! I hope that man pays for what he did."

George said nothing. Maddie interpreted his silence as impact from the night. She said wearily, "Let's head to bed," and then paused for a moment. "How the hell am I going to sleep after *that*?" She looked on the kitchen table and grabbed the bottle of laudanum. Quickly she removed the cap and took a swig. She winked at George and they both headed up to the attic.

George woke the next morning much earlier than usual. It was still pitch black outside. His head felt like a hornets' nest. Thoughts, images and sounds of the last week would not stop, and his eyes moved rapidly under his lids when he closed them.

He decided to get prepared for the day. Better than lying in bed with jangling nerves. After the usual stove stoking and tea making, he headed out to the barn. He thought briefly about hooking up Thunder to the wagon to start, but decided to let the horse rest more. Instead he walked to his wood storage shed and grabbed a couple of planks. After putting a dozen or so in the wagon, he went into the barn and got his toolbox out. The cool morning air was damp, and he wished he had put on his thicker coat. He walked down to Murray creek to get water for the horse, and brought it up to Thunder's stall.

Thunder lifted his head and let out a low whinny. George thought he might have woken him. He gave Thunder some oats by hand, and topped up his hay. While Thunder ate his breakfast, George got the tack out and placed it on the wagon.

A few moments later, light just barely cracking the morning sky, Thunder, George and the wagon rattled to the entrance of Main Street beside Sticky Pete's. George pulled the wagon to a stop. He had not seen the town at this time of the morning for some time. It was silent, some light fog clinging to low spots in the road. And absolutely no light or lamps. George waited and appreciated the stillness.

Then George did hear a sound. A sliding sound, and some light bumping. He recognized the sound as someone moving wood. His first thought was that someone was trying to be quiet so as not to disturb anyone; that did not strike him as right. He quietly pulled the wagon brake in front of the saloon, got off his wagon, and reassured Thunder with a pat. He followed the sound. It was coming from just past the blacksmith.

When George rounded the corner by the blacksmith, he arrived at the build site for the bank. He saw a light wagon parked at the edge of the road, and a hunched figure quietly and slowly removing the wood plank by plank and putting it in the wagon.

George recognized the man. He walked quietly up around his wagon and stood by the back waiting for the man with his next plank. When the man placed the plank, George walked around the wagon and said, "Good morning, Mr. Muces. Up early?"

Mr. Muces froze in place, and looked like he had just swallowed a worm.

George continued. "I don't think that's your wood; it belongs to the bank."

Mr. Muces, looking even more twisted and wrinkled than his sixty-plus years would account for, hissed out, "No bank ever did anyone any good."

George replied, "Who owns the wood really isn't the point, is it? The problem is that it's not yours."

Mr. Muces walked up to George and stood in front of him, making intense eye contact. His fists were clenched and arms held out from his sides like they were ready to punch. He then did a couple of quick movements, trying to fake George into flinching.

For some reason, maybe the lack of sleep, maybe the intensity of the previous night, George felt no fear at all. He felt somewhere between calm and numb. George said, "I am sure the sheriff is going to want to hear about this."

Mr. Muces's face twisted even more; his fists clenched even tighter. He tried one more feint and said, "Asshole," within inches of George's face. George started to laugh at the irony of the insult.

Then, with speed that would be impressive for a man half his age, Mr. Muces leapt onto his wagon, disengaged the brake and whipped the reigns three times in rapid succession. "HYAAA, HYAA, HYAA." The horse and wagon took off.

Unfortunately for Mr. Muces, he had not closed the rear wagon gate or secured the load. The smoothly planed planks slid off the back of his wagon and clattered to the ground. Mr. Muces glanced backwards, noticed he had lost his load, and saw George laughing. He attempted to make a rude gesture with his hands and arm, but in doing so gave the reigns and odd pull, causing his horse to veer sharply to the right. He fell over in his seat but quickly popped up again gaining control of his wagon.

George laughed harder and harder. At first it was the sight of Mr. Muces falling over. Then it was the wood falling out of the wagon. Then it was overhearing Maddie giving Mike hell when he'd been getting Thunder ready.

He doubled over and held on to the woodpile to keep his balance. Then he laughed at the cougar face. Then the sight of Mike's hand disappearing. Then the sight of the door being kicked in with a figure pointing a gun at him. Then he was no longer laughing at anything specific; he was laughing at the ludicrousness of life. The way things could be going along so smoothly one moment, and then absolutely go to shit the next. His stomach got sore. He couldn't stop. Tears were running out of his eyes. He knelt down on the ground gasping, and didn't stop.

Only when he became aware of a large presence next to him did he grab a breath and look up.

Brad was looming over him with a concerned look on his face. "You Okay George?"

George wobbled to his feet. "Oh shit, my horse!" he said. "Brad, I caught Mr. Muces helping himself to the bank's woodpile here just a few minutes ago. But the load slipped out of his wagon when he took off." George started walking back towards Thunder. Brad followed.

"That guy is an absolute shithead," said Brad. "I did the shoes on his horse once when I was new in town. He made up some excuse about a shoddy job and rode away without paying. I never did his horse again. I don't think there is a business in town that hasn't been ripped off by that guy. Even Mr. Service's kid when Service was out on errands. He made up some story about having a tab and took off with fifty bucks worth of goods. With no tab of course.

"And some of the local farmers have been ripped off. Tools—Robert even lost half a pig from his smoker last week." Brad patted George's shoulder. "Would appreciate it if you talked to the sheriff about this. Not many people have caught him stealing; he might be able to do something about it."

George nodded. "I will."

"Speaking of…" said Brad. "How would you like to move that wood into my locked blacksmith building for the weekend. I have some space where I repair wagons and carriages that is empty right now. As long as you get it out first thing Monday, it should be safe."

"Thank you Brad." They walked back with George leading Thunder by the reigns. They talked about the long hot summer. They chatted about the blacksmith business. They talked about George's new quick-building business. They complained some more about Mr. Muces.

"Hey Ho." It was Robert riding Spirit. Both Brad and George waved back. Robert pulled close to the two of them with his horse. "How's the morning going?"

"George here caught old man MEW-KUS trying to take this wood," said Brad.

"Brad has generously donated some locked space for the weekend so it won't disappear," explained George.

Robert got down from his horse and started chatting. "That Muces has been a blight on this area ever since we moved here. He was an original settler; not sure why he has such a hornet in his hat. Caught him wandering around on our west section last week. Claimed he was looking for a lost goat. Then a day later, one of our half-pigs goes missing from the smoker." Robert shrugged.

George then launched into the story about how he'd caught him just this morning—filled with imitations of Mr. Muces and animated arm gestures. By the time he got to the end of the story, all three men were laughing. They continued chatting for a while longer, then Brad said, "Well, these planks aren't going to move themselves." Robert headed on, while

George and Brad loaded the planks into the blacksmith's.

George then got to work on his usual site preparation for the upcoming bank build. He built three workbenches on-site; one was an eight-foot long, smooth-topped workbench for general work. The others were two six-foot benches in perfect line with each other, with jigs on one end for angled cuts. He had refined his build process over the years and had found this one the most efficient.

Mr. Sneed walked over to the build site and wished George a good morning.

"I heard you caught a thief in the act this morning."

"That's true. Word travels fast," replied George.

"I am actually not here about this at all, sir. I had the privilege of talking to your wife a couple of days ago and she mentioned that you are starting a new endeavour." Mr. Sneed smiled that curious smile of his. "Wainwright quick buildings, I believe." George nodded.

"I find this to be quite interesting, and believe it has promise," said Mr. Sneed. "So I have a suggestion for you, one professional to another."

"Okay," said George.

"There is a new type of law called Trademark Law, where you take a name, such as your company name, and you apply the force of law to it. What this does is ensure that no one else can also call their company Wainwright Quick Buildings, and take advantage of your potential success. Or worse, sully your hard-earned reputation."

George gave this some thought. He had a hard time reading Mr. Sneed's true intentions, but decided to listen to his advice. "How much will this cost?"

"Ah yes," replied Mr. Sneed. "The bottom line. It's ten dollars for the initial application and approvals; we send it to Yorktown for processing. Then it's five dollars each year after that to maintain."

"I'll do it," said George.

Mr. Sneed looked surprised at the quick decision. He stood motionless for a moment, and held out his hand. George shook it. "If you can come by the printer's later, I have some papers for you to sign. I will get started on that right now."

George cleaned up the building site, loaded his tools into the wagon, and headed over to the Sheriff's Office.

Maddie saw her husband go into the Sheriff's. She assumed it was follow-up to the events of the prior evening. She walked into the main entrance of the printing company. The typesetter was hunched over a large central press.

As had become his habit, the typesetter, on seeing Maddie walk in, started complaining about his work. "I am not going to last with all this hunching." He straightened up and stretched his back with a look of pain. "Thankless job this, producing a local paper and the occasional *wanted* sign for pennies a job. Never make much money. Just enough for a sad meal once in a while."

Maddie nodded sympathetically.

The man squinted at Maddie. "And how can I help you today?"

"I wanted to find out how much it would cost to get a bunch of posters printed." Maddie put one of the posters she had made for George on the table. The printer hunched over and looked closely at the poster.

"Well, I can't replicate the type style of some of these strokes; we are limited to the five fonts shown over here." He pointed to a small framed poster on the wall with a few rows of type on it demonstrating both font and size.

Maddie took a close look. "I think a couple of these will do. What do you do if you need to create type that does not look like any of these?"

"You would have to buy more type from the supplier; a set of type is not cheap at all. Even a print run of a thousand copies wouldn't pay for it. Or... if you are that way inclined, some printers carve their own letters for special runs for an additional charge. But... I am not that way inclined."

Maddie nodded. She looked around the print shop and noticed some colourful posters on the wall.

"How do these get made?"

"You are full of questions today!" The printer then stretched himself further and showed Maddie a group of colourful inkpots. "That's for the screen printer. Print that needs more pictures, colour, and simple text can be made this way."

Maddie nodded. "How does it work?"

The printer looked at Maddie and looked at the machine. "Well, the first step is to create some stencils to mask out the areas..."

Later that day, George and Maddie were working together to pull firewood down from the hills behind their cabin ready to be cut to length. Winter was coming, and a good stock of firewood could be the difference between life and freezing to death.

They would pull full-length, topped trees with the branches trimmed down beside the barn ready to be cut to length for the stove. It was easier to cut them on the sawhorses created for that purpose by the barn than cut them up in the woods. Sometimes, they would work together hauling a single large tree down to the barn. And occasionally, for the largest trees, Thunder would help out with the hauling.

All this work would result in lots of debris, but both Maddie and George put a lot of effort into keeping their homestead neat and organized. So Maddie started a fire in their firepit outside that was kept going with the bark and branches throughout the day.

Once the sun started setting, Maddie brought out some bread and some thick chunks of pork with the rind still attached. They would place these pork chunks on the end of a stick, and roast them over the firepit, allowing the melting fat to drip down the pork and, once the pork was thoroughly covered, the same drips would add flavour to their bread. Especially after an afternoon of physical labour, this was a welcome meal.

"I saw you go into the sheriff's today," said Maddie. "You know, I think that man should hang for what he tried to do to you. That was attempted murder."

"I was in the Sheriff's Office for something else," said George evasively. "I caught old man Muces helping himself to that pile of wood on the bank job. I wanted to fill out a statement so that the sheriff could follow up. Muces nearly crashed his wagon!"

Maddie recognized his attempt at steering the conversation. "George," she said in a low warning tone, "what happened at the Sheriff's Office last night?"

George avoided Maddie's gaze. "It turns out Mike was a wanted man. Did some thefts at a hotel and some other places. Because some of it was worth more than a hundred dollars, he is going to jail."

Maddie's voice was now calm and measured. George knew this was an indicator of a potential explosion. She asked, "George, you did tell the sheriff what happened here last night?"

Maddie stood up and kept moving into George's line of vision whenever he attempted to look away. George looked at the fire for a moment, reached inside his jacket and pulled out the flask given to him by Robert. He said quickly, "I told the sheriff it was a drunken shotgun accident." He held out the flask, straight-armed, in the direction of Maddie.

Maddie exploded. "George! Sometimes I think you are just *too damn soft*! That man pointed a gun at your head and was about to kill you! About to murder you! Dead! Wipe you out! *Why, George, why*?"

George replied, holding Maddie's gaze. "I knew he was going to jail. He doesn't have a right hand anymore, Maddie. It didn't feel right."

Maddie grabbed the glass flask from George's hand and took a simply massive swig. George saw the hairs on her arm stand on end, saw the look on her face, and knew the moonshine was having its effect. Maddie breathed out, "Yhhhhhhhhaaaaaaaawwwwwww." Tears were running down her face from the strength of the shine.

"What is wrong with you, George? You are literally letting a man get away with murder!" She emphasized the words with arms flailing and paced in front of George.

George looked down at the ground, and, after a moment, looked back up at Maddie. "Do you remember shooting Mike?"

"Of course I remember shooting Mike!"

"Why did you shoot him in the hand instead of his head?"

Maddie looked confused and frustrated. "Fuck off, George."

George replied, "The reason you didn't drop him on the spot is the same reason I didn't send him to the hangman."

Maddie was furious. She took a more measured swig of the moonshine and stared at George. George did not look away. Maddie stormed into the cabin, slamming the door behind her.

JUNCTION 1882

PART TWO

CHAPTER 15

THE SPRING OF '82 WAS EVEN MORE welcome than usual; a long cold winter had left many locals in a foul mood as cabin fever had set in. Even a trip to Sticky Pete's was not in the cards when the weather outside was below thirty and the wind was howling.

George's new business was doing well. It now offered three different styles of buildings: the original design; an L-shaped building called "The Trappers Cabin," and an extended-height version that had a stand-up attic which could be used as an extra room (bedroom usually) or extra storage. As George had hoped, he was now able to work full time in Junction, on building kits or local work, so didn't have to travel into Yorktown. He contemplated building a dedicated workshop for the business, including an area to season wood, but didn't have quite the business to justify the expense.

Maddie had taken over the print shop, and had found great interest in two specific pursuits. The first was writing the local newspaper. She started a popular monthly piece called "Farmer's Corner" that discussed the weather over the last month, what was going well for local farmers, and what wasn't. When local farmers banded together to buy a steam tractor, she spent a couple of evenings carving a tiny picture of a steam tractor in a

wood block so that the paper would have the image to accompany the story. She would also write stories on locals and local events.

Maddie started making colourful screen prints, sometimes of local subjects, some that looked like embroidery with sayings of wisdom included. Within a few months, most businesses and many of the local houses had at least one Maddie print on the walls.

Sticky Pete's also ran a weekly advertising section in the Junction paper that told of special events, music, and what the weekly food was. The paper had such success that Maddie was selling a hundred every week to Yorktown. Which Pete didn't mind at all, because some curious Yorktown locals would head out for a bowl of stew and a drink on a day trip to Junction.

Pete had hired some extra help, a one-armed man called John Cooper who helped out part time around the saloon with cleaning and small repairs. John did small jobs around town and also volunteered at the church.

Mr. Sneed had become a trusted part of the community, not only as a banker but a financial adviser and trademark and patent officer. He continued to rent the floor above the print shop, giving Maddie the monthly rent, as there was no residence in the bank and he appreciated the central location and low rent.

Not much was seen of Mr. Muces after he was given a twenty-dollar fine for theft by the sheriff. Things did sometimes still go missing however, mostly focused in rural areas.

Robert had reluctantly yielded to his boys and partnered with some other local farmers on the purchase of a steam tractor. This was on the condition that his sons took over responsibility for the wheat operation, and he solely focused on raising cattle. His sons bought another section of land as they now had increased farming capacity.

The yearly harvest labour rush was lighter now, half of what it used to be. However, the station at Junction had been expanded. It now included a yard tower, three long storage tracks and a passing track. This supported growing freight operations. Pete had been concerned about the loss of harvest business, but between train personnel, a growing town, and visitors from Yorktown, he did just fine.

CHAPTER 16

JJ PAUSED BY THE BUDS of a small maple tree. The lower buds and shoots were chewed back, the work of the local deer population. He had been disappointed by his day in the mountains; the wolf population had shrunk, most likely due to hunting pressure. The Blue Mountains' close proximity to Yorktown meant they were being well hunted. Most hunters did not have the skill to catch wolves, which, on the one hand meant his wolf pelts got a handsome price, but on the other hand, frequently-hunted deer were a wolf food source, putting pressure on their population.

So seeing some signs of deer was good, but he recognized the change that was happening.

He had tried to be a hunting guide, but he had no tolerance for the ineptitude of city hunters. They had no concept of being silent or minimizing impact, crashing and cracking through the woods with cumbersome boots and preferring to chat and drink loudly over any actual hunting. One of them once took a pot-shot at a Great Horned Owl, and hit it. He had watched the magnificent bird spiral down from the sky. That was the last hunting trip he led.

He looked at new shoots pushing up through the ground, recognizing some as wild onions and making note of their location. He harvested some wild herbs, always being sure to take just enough to allow them to continue to flourish.

When he arrived at the Blue River, he walked upstream to a large tree that he had felled into a makeshift bridge. It was against his nature to cut such a tree down for this purpose, but a hard lesson a few years ago when he had broken through the ice, left him wanting a four-season way to cross the river, unpassable right now with spring floods. He had contemplated building a boat, but didn't like the idea of leaving it unattended by the river with more hunters of questionable nature around. And he didn't like boats.

He crossed the river and walked soundlessly through the fresh spring grass towards his cabin. Last fall, he had worked with George on upgrading the cabin, and he was very glad he had. While well built, the single layer of sheathing did not provide much insulation in deep winter, especially out in the open like his was. They had added an inside wall stuffed with horsehair from the livery, along with an additional layer on the ceiling stuffed with the same. George had suggested doubling the windows, which they did, by simply attaching a second two-by-two window inside the first. Local clay from beside the river mixed with horsehair blocked all drafts.

He stopped walking and froze. He could hear the sound of clinking and rummaging in the cabin. He knew by the sounds that it was not small animals, and by the sound and smell that it wasn't a bear. He quietly pulled the rifle sling on his back around his body so that the rifle was now in front. He slipped it out of its sling and placed the stock against his shoulder. Raising the barrel, he pulled back the hammer.

He walked up to the cabin and noticed the door had been forced. He used the gun barrel to gently push the well-oiled door open.

Mr. Muces felt the change in wind and light and quickly turned around. He remarked weakly, "Oh, this is your cabin?"

JJ replied, "Hello Jack," and shot him straight through the head, killing him instantly.

CHAPTER 17

MADDIE AND GEORGE SELDOM SPOKE about either the cougar incident or Mike. Maddie would dismissively refer to it as "hell week" before changing the subject if it ever came up. However, Maddie refused to ride or take the wagon past the hardwood forest beside the farm. And they both would have nightmares about the events—sometimes, one of them would wake up to the sound of the other moaning and talking in the strange, distorted language of dreams. This would lead to the other saying, "It's okay. You're here at home. You are safe. It's okay."

One morning, they were both eating hearty bowls of oats when George turned to Maddie.

"Thank you."

Maddie said, "For what?"

"Waking me up last night. I was in the middle of..."

"No problem, no problem," said Maddie, waving the conversation topic away. "So today is the day! We finally find out what the mystery 'opportunities' are!"

"True, true," said George, looking at the three telegrams on the table. He read the first one out loud.

"George Wainwright. I have two business opportunities. Interested? Hope you and wife are well. Chamberlain. STOP."

"And today we find out what they are!" said Maddie. "Exciting! Are you nervous?"

"A bit, definitely. I am already pretty stretched with what I have going on, and don't want to commit to something I can't do," said George.

"Neither do I," said Maddie. "I like having you around here a bit more."

"But you could be rich!" said George, a bit sarcastically.

Maddie stood up and kissed him on the cheek.

George stood and made sure he had not spilled any oats on his best clothes. Maddie brushed his clothes to remove any wrinkles and bits of dirt. "Looking good!"

George decided to walk into town rather than take the horse. It made it easier to keep his clothes clean, and he liked to clear his head before talking business.

He first walked to the bank, and took a moment to appreciate it. It was a good-looking building with a white and dark-green colour scheme, fancy trim on the front, and signs on the front and windows, painted by Maddie. George walked up to the front door, and was surprised to find it locked.

"George. George!" Brad's voice came from the blacksmith's next door. George walked over. "Mr. Sneed was already here this morning to get his papers. He is going to meet you at Sticky Pete's."

"Thank you, Brad."

George walked into Sticky Pete's. On seeing him, Pete walked over and said, "I hear you are having some business meetings this morning."

"Word travels fast," replied George.

"If you need Room Six, just let me know," said Pete. Room Six was a non-bed hotel room that was reserved for private business conversations. It functioned as both Pete's office and a good place to discuss business with out-of-towners.

George nodded. "Thank you Pete." Pete gave a small salute and walked back behind the bar. Kat brought over a hot cup of tea. George nodded his thanks. Kat gave a quick smile.

Suddenly, the saloon doors swung open and Mr. Service came rushing in. He looked around the saloon, saw George, and ran over to sit immediately opposite him.

George said cautiously, "Hello, Mr. Service?"

Mr. Service replied, "Sorry George, hate to rush like this, but I heard you have a couple of business meetings this morning."

"It seems everyone has."

Mr. Service continued. "I know you are probably going to get lots of new work out of your meetings this morning, so wanted to get myself in first so that I could be higher on the list." Mr. Service looked awkwardly at George.

George said, "It's okay. Probably not necessary, as I prioritize good friends over most things. But continue."

Mr. Service relaxed visibly. "I met with Sneed a week or so ago about getting a loan together for some business expansion. My goal has always been to try and serve Junction with my

Mercantile, so that people do not need to travel to Yorktown for supplies. Well, recently I have realized that my problem isn't storage anymore. It's simply that my store isn't big enough." He paused while George had a sip of his tea.

"So I want to open a second store, one dedicated to food only. My current store will become Service Hardware. And the second will become a grocer. And I want to get the best, most honest builder there is." Mr. Service smiled broadly. "So what do you say, buddy, you in?"

George smiled back. "Of course!"

Mr. Service grabbed his hand and shook it enthusiastically. "Thank you sir!" he said, and left the saloon as quickly as he'd come in. George sat back in his chair and laughed. He was looking forward to this job. It was a manageable size and he loved building in his own town.

The next person to arrive was Mr. Sneed. His suit was perfectly pressed, buttons polished to a high standard, absolutely everything in place, as George knew it would be. He placed a brown leather satchel on the seat beside George and headed over to the counter. He asked Kat, "How recently was the coffee brewed?"

Kat replied, "It's been busy this mornin', about ten minutes ago."

"One cup of black coffee," stated Mr. Sneed. He walked back over to the table and sat down, sitting in perfect posture.

"Good Morning Mr. Sneed," said George. "Thank you for coming." Mr. Sneed gave a slight nod in response. They both sat there, sipping their beverages for a few minutes, until George got up and wandered out to the veranda. He knew that the visitors were most likely arriving by train, so he took advantage of the saloon's view of the station.

The train's whistle bubbled and blasted forth as it approached the crossing and station. Attached to the back of the train was an unusual sight: a business car. This car was much better appointed than most of the train cars and was usually reserved for train executives and dignitaries.

Once the train had stopped, a porter dressed in blue emerged from the business car and placed a wooden stepping block at the base of the stairs. He scaled the stairs at the back of the car and opened the door. Three well-dressed gentlemen emerged from the car and headed down the stairs.

A horse and carriage had been waiting at the corner of the station platform. It drew up to the platform and the porter opened the door to the carriage. George laughed, as the station could not be more than five minutes' walk from the saloon.

The carriage pulled up in front of the saloon and the door was carefully opened by the driver. George sipped his tea. The driver wasn't quite sure what to do with the swinging saloon doors, so he held them open the best he could as the three men went inside, completely ignoring George.

They noticed Mr. Sneed, however, and the three walked up to him. One extended his hand and said, "Mr. Wainwright, I presume?"

Mr. Sneed stood up as George walked over. "No. I am Mr. Sneed, Mr. Wainwright's banker and advisor. This is Mr. Wainwright." He indicated George.

"You are Mr. Wainwright?" one of them asked incredulously. "The one recommended by Mr. Chamberlain?"

"In the flesh," George said, extending his hand. One of the men took it and shook it.

The man who shook his hand said, "I am John Roebuck, and this is my banker, Mr. Shmidt, and my lawyer, Mr. Capper."

"His financial advisor," corrected Mr. Shmidt. He turned to Mr. Capper and said quietly with a wry smile, "Perhaps we have made a mistake; perhaps our offer is a bit generous?" Mr. Capper and Mr. Shmidt both snickered.

Mr. Capper turned back to Mr. Shmidt and said quietly, "Is it too late to remove a zero?" they both chuckled. John Roebuck looked at them with dismay and signalled towards the table. "Shall we sit, gentlemen?"

Mr. Capper made eye contact with George for the first time that day and pulled a paper from his bag. "This is a contract to purchase your company's trade name for"—he paused for effect—"two *hundred* and fifty dollars." He slid it across the table to George.

The banker then spoke. "This shouldn't take but minutes; I mean, this is a once-in-a-lifetime offer, unless we were beaten to the punch by a parade of other senior banking partners." Mr. Capper and Mr. Shmidt starting snickering again.

George looked over at John, and noticed he looked slightly embarrassed. George asked him, "So, you are John Roebuck, one of the partners of the famous catalogue firm that most of us order our goods from?"

"The one and only!" said Mr. Shmidt with a flourish.

"Thank you Shmidt. I can answer my own questions," said John quietly but firmly. He turned back to George. "I am the son of the Roebuck you are thinking of, in charge of a few new catalogue divisions." He thought for a moment. "You see, we have an excess of..."

"I strongly advise you to stop right there!" stated the lawyer. "He does not need to know the details; I am sure he is quite willing to sign for such a generous sum!" He pulled out a pen and inkpot, put them on the table, opened the pot, dipped the pen, and gave the contract to George to sign.

George did not take the pen. He looked back at John. "So, I take it you are therefore in charge of this meeting, and are"—George cleared his throat—"the boss of these two gentlemen." Both the lawyer and the banker bristled at such a suggestion.

The lawyer said, "I will not sit here and..."

John interrupted. "Yes, you will."

George asked John, "Can we go and discuss this ourselves away from these men? There is a business room upstairs that is set up for just such a purpose."

The banker squeaked, "This is most unusual and I do not recommend…"

"Agreed," said John, glaring at both his banker and lawyer. George took the paper that had been passed to him and passed it across to Mr. Sneed. "Can you take a look at this in detail and let me know if there is anything I should be wary of? And what exactly the contract is selling these men?"

Mr. Sneed smiled politely and took the contract. "Will do, sir."

George said, "Follow me," to John, and they walked past the bar. George called out to Pete, "We are going up to Room Six. Can you bring me a beer and Mr. Roebuck a…"

Mr. Roebuck replied, "Whiskey, double."

Pete nodded and passed them the room key. They both headed upstairs while Mr. Sneed examined the contract closely. Both Mr. Shmidt and Mr. Capper sat in their chairs with their arms crossed, looking very angry.

CHAPTER 18

JJ STOOD AT THE DOOR to his cabin looking across the land. He was watching to see if his gunshot had drawn any attention, any signs of horse or human movement. He supposed that a gunshot by the heavily hunted Blue Mountains would not draw much attention, but needed to be sure.

He had bound his victim's wrists together tightly, and bent the legs, binding the ankles to the thighs. He sipped some water and waited a few more minutes at the door of the cabin.

He then went inside, and heaved Mr. Muces onto his back. He threaded his head between the bound arms, and pulled the body until its armpits lined up with his shoulders. He then bound the wrists to his body like a belt to hold the body firmly in position. The bound legs would not dangle down the back, giving him more freedom of movement. He grabbed a blanket and flung it over his back, pulling the two corners over his shoulders and tucking them in his front. He took a pair of small leather shoes and a small tin and put them in one of his pockets.

He again paused at the cabin door, and rapidly headed back to the Blue River. To anyone viewing from a distance, he would simply look like a man carrying a large blanket-covered pack.

He moved across the river and along its far bank at a pace much faster than usual. His normally attentive gaze was not focused on all of the signs the land provided him, but instead on detecting any other human presence and his rapid motion.

He got to a small stream that emptied into the river, swollen and brown with spring runoff. He turned up this stream and started following it towards the looming mountain that was its source. Within half an hour or so, the going started to get much tougher: the path was steep, thin, rocky and slippery with water spray. He focused intensely on his foot placement, making sure each one was well positioned on solid, secure ground.

The path started heading up steeply beside the creek; within short order he was fifty or so feet above its rushing waters. He found a spot dried by sunlight and paused for a moment. The path ahead of him turned into a goat trail, six inches wide at its widest, and for some sections not existing at all. He took a long hard look back down the trail and listened carefully.

Satisfied that he was not being followed, he shifted his weight and took off the heavy blanket now saturated with water. He placed it on a warm sunny rock. He then sat down and took off his boots, his socks steaming from moisture in the cool spring air. He removed them as well and hung them on a small branch.

Reaching in his pocket, he took out the small tin and tiny leather shoes. After allowing his feet to dry, he opened the tin and sprinkled talcum on both his feet and inside the shoes. Rolling the shoes like socks, he placed them on his toes and unrolled them onto his feet. He bound them tightly to his ankles with some thin leather straps. He did the same to the cuffs of his pants. He stood up, shifting the body on his back until it was centred. He puffed a couple of touches of talc on his hands, rubbed them together and put the tin away.

He looked up the impossible trail and carefully chose his first foothold.

CHAPTER 19

JOHN ROEBUCK LEANED BACK in his chair in Room 6 and took a long draw from his whiskey. A smile spread on his face.

"You know, this is the first time today I have felt truly relaxed. I was surrounded by the finest of luxury in that train car of my father's, but... the company!"

George laughed.

John spoke further. "And I must apologize for my two associates downstairs. They were not chosen by me; they were appointed to me at the last minute. I had anticipated coming out on my own. Or with one of my own associates. They do not necessarily speak for me."

"Understood," said George, now taking a sip of his beer.

Over the next twenty minutes not one word of business was discussed. They talked about their towns, their homes. John talked about his three homes: one in the west, one on the east coast, and one down south for the winter months. George talked about how much he loved his town, how he had watched it grow, and some of the local adventures, including Mr. Muces attempting to steal the wood and nearly crashing. And how another time he was in his workshop chuckling while his wife was giving another man hell. "I may have even stayed a moment or two longer than necessary," said George.

John appreciated the local stories and humour, and laughed heartily. He seemed like a man who did not get many opportunities to loosen up. George appreciated John's honesty, and his sharing about how sometimes, moving three times a year was not the best choice for his family. George talked about how he had started his business so he could be home more, and not have to go to Yorktown when work was thin. He then asked John about his business with him.

"As I was saying downstairs, our company has run into a small challenge. Nothing I am not up for, mind you," said John, looking straight into George's eyes.

"We are the premier shipper of catalogue products on this continent; no one else even comes close to what we move. Clothing, appliances, medicines and dry goods—you name it.. So, we are looking to expand into other markets."

George nodded.

"We have purchased a number of interests in lumber operations, mills, and other related industries in anticipation of being able to sell the resulting products through our catalogue. But, in all honesty, they have flopped. No one thinks of our catalogue when they think of wood-based building supplies. Nails, sure. Windows and wood, no. So, I noticed a few weeks ago your prepared building kits and thought this might be the answer for us."

George nodded again.

"However, we have a brand problem. We already know our brand is not associated with wood-based building products. However, yours is. So, if we could purchase your brand, and say, your reputation as such, then we could get a head start on our operations."

George and John proceeded to discuss the details of such an arrangement and, in what felt like a few minutes, an hour had passed.

John took the last sip of his whiskey and had another hearty laugh. "You know what," he said, "fuck it. I have these goddamn ten-dollar Cuban cigars; we were supposed to smoke them in victory on the way back in the train while laughing at the cheap price we got your name for. At least that was my associates' plan. But I would much rather smoke them here with you and enjoy just a few more moments' peace." Both men did just that, appreciating the smoothness of the cigars and lack of pretension in their company.

When George and John descended the curving stairs of the saloon, they saw that just Mr. Sneed remained, so they joined him at the table. Mr. Sneed stated the obvious: "The other men have left, back to the train, I believe."

"What is your conclusion on the contract?" Asked George.

"It's a fairly standard legal contract, but three things I think will concern you. The first is that you lose the rights to your own name, You would have to rename your company."

George nodded. Sneed continued, "And, also of concern to you would be the complete lack of quality control. They could put out anything of any quality and have your name on it. And thirdly,"—Mr. Sneed looked directly at George for emphasis—"I believe that your name is considerably undervalued."

"He is very good," said Mr. Roebuck. "I can see why you trust him. Now, if I can just find an advisor that can so well represent my interests, and not just their own. Well, George, Mr. Sneed, I must be on my way—always someone else to meet." He rolled his eyes slightly. He leaned in closer to George, stating, "And very sorry we could not come to an agreeable arrangement." He stood up and shook both men's hands.

As he walked outside, he spoke briefly to the porter. "I will walk to the station, thank you."

CHAPTER 20

JJ TURNED AND FACED his body to the rock surface. He reached up with his hands and felt the smooth surface for handholds. Once secure, he moved each foot carefully, placing most of his weight on the big toe or ball of his foot. He moved slowly and deliberately, completely focused on the task at hand. He had completed this route once before, with a wolf pelt in his pack, so he knew it was feasible. And as this was the sunny side of the canyon, most rock surfaces were dry. But the slightly shifting weight of a man on his back made it much more challenging.

He had first discovered this area when the creek was dry a couple of summers ago. While still tough going, the creek bed made a considerably easier and safer path than this. It was also possible in deep winter, where wolf tracks and deer tracks up the frozen creek trail had captured his attention.

Now, however, he was a hundred feet above the roaring creek. And about halfway along the goat trail. One of his footholds suddenly gave way, the rocks clattering down the sheer wall to the creek below. His hands held tight to the narrow rock ledge he had been creeping them along. He hung there for a moment, straight armed, and scanned the wall ahead of him. A short, sharp rock point protruded up at an angle to his right.

He shifted his weight to his right and placed his big toe on the point, hooking his toe to grab it. He simultaneously pulled with his right hand and toe, shifting his weight over the point. The rock point pushed its way through the leather shoe and into his toe. Shots of pain travelled up his leg.

JJ was not unfamiliar with pain, however, and knew it also meant his footing was secure. He proceeded up the other half of the goat trail until it started widening out. Here he took a pause, and shook out his arms and legs. He looked out across the alpine valley before him. It was lush and green, with coniferous forest filling both sides of the creek bed. Further up, the valley had clusters of snow, with a snow-covered glacier capping the end, the source of the creek for most of the year.

He worked his way down to the valley floor and found what he was looking for, a narrow path used by wolves when patrolling their territory. He had seen a pregnant female a couple of weeks earlier and knew this was a critical time for her to find food. If he had known the female was present and pregnant, he wouldn't have shot her mate.

"Here ya go!" He said to the lone female wolf, swinging the body onto the ground beside the path. "That should keep you all going for a while."

He took a moment to look at the body. "Fuck you, Jack."

CHAPTER 21

WELL, HOW DID THAT GO?" asked Pete after wandering over to their table. "You rich now? You leaving this town?" he joked.

"Not a chance. On either one," said George smiling.

"Well, hope you both worked up an appetite, because I have steak on the grill with eggs this morning. And it is, if I do say so myself, *tasty*!"

"Sign me up!" said George, banging his cup on the table for emphasis.

"I too would like to try that," said Mr. Sneed.

Pete walked with haste over to the kitchen. Just a few minutes later he walked back over with two plates, each with a thick steak, three eggs on top, and a generous pile of hash browns. Kat brought over cutlery and topped up Mr. Sneed's coffee.

"Wow," said George, and without hesitation tucked in. Mr. Sneed followed suit, with smaller, well-considered portions and bites.

Just as George was taking in his fourth or fifth bite, he felt a hand on his shoulder. "Mr. Wainwright, I presume?"

He looked up, steak still in his mouth, and saw two men standing behind him in flannel shirts. "Oh crap! Sorry!" he said, quickly wiping his mouth and swallowing.

"Oh, don't worry. That looks tasty, wouldn't mind some myself!" said one of the men.

"Pete!" called out George, "Two more!" Pete looked back and gave a quick salute.

One of the men held out his hand. "Mr. McLeod." George held out his hand and got a very firm handshake. "And this is my money man, Mr. Missoura. He keeps me on track," he said winking. George got another firm handshake.

"And this is my banker, Mr. Sneed," said George. Mr. Sneed shook both men's hands. Pete walked over with two more plates and placed them on the table, with cutlery rapidly following. Kat put two mugs on the table and filled them with coffee.

"Now *this* is the way to start a meeting!" said Mr. McLeod.

Both men started tucking in with vigour. "So, as you probably know, I am McLeod, of McLeod and McLeod Forestry," he said with his mouth full.

"I have seen your name on the train cars passing here," said George.

"The other McLeod is not here today because he is feeling... under the weather!" Mr. McLeod's huge laugh surged forth, and the other three men joined, as much in response to Mr. McLeod's huge laugh as the joke.

Mr. Sneed cringed at the sight of the men's open mouths with half-finished contents, but did his best to hide it.

"Well, my *money man* here," said Mr. McLeod, clapping Mr. Missoura on the back, "has informed me that we are not making as much money as we could." Mr. Missoura nodded.

McLeod continued. "Every spring we set up new logging camps all over this fine land. And we set 'em up with canvas tents and a fresh batch of workers." His jaw worked furiously on the steak. "And as we move through the woods, cuttin' only the biggest and straightest trees, we move the camp. No sense having workers spending their time going on hikes through the woods when they could be working. You follow so far?"

George nodded.

"So, it's all moving along fine and dandy, then fall comes along, then winter. And it all goes to crap!" Mr. McLeod leaned into George. George could hear his furious chewing. "Half my labourers or more leave because of the weather. I mean, sure the conditions for work are tougher, but the work keeps you warm. The crappy canvas tents, however, get saturated and frozen, and don't hold heat at all, even less in blizzards. So I lose most of my workforce— some good workers too!"

McLeod leaned back and looked at George. "Can you see where I am going with this, son? Can you *see*?"

George nodded rapidly, his enthusiasm building. "I do, I do! You want some of my quick buildings so that you can log the sites with a full workforce all year!"

McLeod smiled. "Smart man, this one," he said, looking at Mr. Missoura. "And we want to put them on skids, so that we can move 'em with the steam donkey when we move camp. You see, we can build log cabins; we sure have enough logs!" He nudged George. "But that takes paid time away from the work crew, and they are a lot harder to move. Especially the mess hall, it's forty feet long. You ain't movin' that!"

George sat up in his seat with excitement. "I think I can help you even further!"

McLeod smiled. "Lay it on me son, lay it on me!"

"I can build the buildings so that they can come apart. Build the walls so that they can be taken apart in one piece! That way, you can not only move them, but pack them out on a train when you are moving to a different camp. And... and..."

McLeod forked another generous piece of steak into his mouth and leaned into George, both men building up excitement.

"You can build your mess hall the same way; it's just like three or four of my buildings end to end, with the modular walls!" George's face lit up with excitement.

"Godammit, man—that is frickin' genius! *Genius*, I say." McLeod took in a deep breath. "Hold it, hold it, let me check in with the boss first." He turned to his money man. "Does that work?"

Mr. Missoura looked up from the last bite of his steak and appeared thoughtful. "I think so," he said, "we have yet to discuss cost, however."

"Well discuss cost, man. I got steak to finish," McLeod boomed.

Mr. Missoura started, "We would need, say, twenty units by fall. Can you do that?"

George nodded.

Missoura continued. "And we would expect a pretty significant discount at that volume."

George answered, "If you can provide me with the lumber to build the cabins, I can give them to you at thirty percent off. If you don't need the windows, then forty percent. My work is still worth something."

Mr. McLeod laughed. "*If* we can provide you the lumber. Sir, we cut that much in a *day!* And mill it in the same. *If* we can provide that much—please!"

All four men laughed.

Mr. Missoura said, "I think we can get away with one window a cabin, and provide you with all the wood needed for twenty cabins."

"And one mess hall," said George.

"And *two* mess halls. And give each mess hall two windows, we are not frickin' *barbarians* here!" said Mr. McLeod, a piece of hash brown sailing from his mouth over the table towards Mr. Sneed, who deftly moved his head laterally to dodge it.

All the men but Mr. Sneed laughed uproariously.

After catching his breath, Missoura spoke. "So the equivalent of twenty-six cabins' worth of wood?"

George nodded, adding, "And one window per cabin. How's thirty-five percent off the regular price sound?"

"DEAL!" boomed McLeod. "Oh, crap!" he said. He looked at Mr. Missoura. "Deal?"

Mr. Missoura smiled. "All done by end of August. Deal."

All the men shook hands and tucked into the last of their meals.

George turned to Mr. Sneed. "Can you write up a contract to cover this? Include the total board feet of wood, plus the dimensions and windows, and give it to Mr. Missoura for review?"

Mr. Sneed nodded.

Mr. McLeod noticed that Mr. Sneed had not finished his meal. "You not gonna finish that, son?" he boomed.

Mr. Sneed said weakly, "Oh, I already had a big breakfast."

All the men laughed again.

"Well!" said Mr. McLeod, standing up and wiping his mouth with his flannel shirt. "No rest for the wicked!"

Mr. Missoura stood up and headed to the door with his boss. On their way out, Mr. McLeod shouted to Mr. Missoura, "Best DAMN business meeting I ever had! We should schedule more over meals like that!"

Mr. Sneed turned to George. "Can you *not* invite me to that?"

George headed up the trail to his cabin, deciding to go through the poplar grove. The light green leaves filtered the sunlight and left the area feeling fresh and new. He marvelled at how fast the new poplar growth was, some of it six inches of growth in just the last couple of weeks. The forest floor was covered in new green shoots, and a couple of pines were just starting to push through the undergrowth. The pine buds had started to crack, shedding their papery brown cases.

He was surprised how tired his body and mind felt. He could spend ten hours in the workshop and not feel as tired as he did after three hours of business meetings. He did feel good and full; his massive breakfast had taken care of that.

A shot rang out and echoed through the woods. It came from the cabin. George sprinted through the rest of the grove, and up to the cabin. He ripped open the cabin door. "Maddie? Maddie?" He moved quickly through the cabin, then out the back door. He looked towards the barn and saw Maddie there, shotgun in hand, standing at the corner.

Her gaze was intently on the woods behind the barn. George walked up behind her. "Maddie?"

She turned and saw his face. "Don't worry. A black bear was sniffing around the barn and worrying Thunder. I scared him off. He took off into the woods." She smiled.

They walked back to the cabin. "So, how was the morning? Are we rich?" she asked jokingly.

"Not rich, maybe, but I am more than double booked till fall," George replied.

"Don't tell me any more!" she said. "I want to hear all of the details over tea."

"Sure," said George. "Looking forward to sitting down, honestly. With no bar sounds or businessmen."

"But it does look like I am going to be building a new shop," George said, stepping up to the cabin.

Maddie thought for a moment. "So I can finally get a new rug for the front room! Can you do something for me?"

"Most likely," replied George

"Can you build the new shop on the other side of our section? I mean, it's nice having you close and all, but other workers and men, not really."

"I think that's a good idea," said George. "I am also going to have to buy a steam donkey, so it's probably going to be pretty noisy."

They walked inside, and Maddie put the kettle on the stove, opening the cast-iron door on the front to stoke it.

"Okay, so, tell me all the details. Who did you meet? What were they like?"

CHAPTER 22

JJ'S TRIP BACK FELT LIKE he was floating. The weight off his back meant he could traverse the cliff face slowly, lightly, moving smoothly like a cat. He enjoyed it so much he contemplated trying an even harder route, but then remembered he had a couple of tasks that needed to be done in short order.

He travelled back through the forest feeling alive, like smells were stronger and clearer, the light showed more detail and colour, and the endless signs that the woods provided came in clear and without confusion.

His afternoon flowed smoothly from there, until he forgot how much more complicated replacing two boards with bullet holes in them could be when horsehair was stuffed between them. The day had been going so well, he had assumed when he held a second board in place to prevent the horsehair from coming down as he pried out the first, that it would just... work. Instead, horsehair poured out of the small space he had left below the board and coated his cabin floor and possessions with a generous layer.

Instead of being able to enjoy a small relaxed meal over his fire as was his plan, he spent the afternoon pulling apart his bedding and cleaning out the cabin of horsehair, sweeping and hand brushing every nook and corner to remove it.

Then shaking out all his clothes and bedding to get rid of it.

He was irritated by the time he finished up, and found no solace in chewing some dried meat and berry mix he had made months earlier. He had also pried up the floorboards that were blood covered and burned those in the fire. Hammering out and straightening the now-rusty nails from those boards and re-using them to attach the new floorboards was also frustrating; they bent more easily and were harder to pound in due to the rough surface on the nails.

JJ's mood had utterly changed from the light, alive feeling he'd had when he arrived at his cabin, to an agitated one that made him throw his hammer in fury before retrieving it from the grass in frustration.

He started imagining how he could finish up the day. Maybe a second check of his traps close to the river—the rabbits were active and he might have some already? Maybe a sit and a smoke while he sat by the raging river and soaked in the sounds and smells? Perhaps process another skin, stretch it a bit further and remove any remnants left on the backside? Maybe just a sit and contemplation in his cabin?

Then he sat up straight and a smile spread over his face. It was poker night at Sticky Pete's! There was beer, good conversation, music and friends! Feeling immediately better, he started the hour-long trek to the saloon.

CHAPTER 23

PETE STOOD UP AND stretched his back after filling the shelves behind the bar with row after row of glasses. The last of his dinner customers were at the front of the saloon, drinking beer and talking, long after finishing their meals. He had tapped a new keg, readying for the anticipated full house of the night.

He had no idea that the poker night would become the success it had. It started out as a single table in the corner. He had expanded it to a high-roller and smaller-stakes table after locals became discouraged when out-of-town sharks would dominate. The sharks naturally gravitated to the higher-stakes table. He kept expanding as demand grew, bringing in music, hiring dealers in exchange for drinks, meals and sometimes a room. His once-a-month Thursday was now busier than most Saturdays.

He watched as Kathy and John removed the smaller tables from the expansive main floor of the saloon, and brought in the eight-foot round tables that were used for poker night. They worked with practised efficiency, moving the chairs to the side, removing the smaller tables, bringing in the new tables, wiping them down and setting up the chairs. John had been a good addition to the bar, despite his single arm. He showed up every day on time, clean shaven and clean cut, and he cleaned and prepped the rooms to a higher standard than anyone else had. He was a bit shy with customers, but Kathy more than made up for that. If things kept going the way they were, then he might be able to afford to bump him to full time. Pete could use some more help in the kitchen.

Things looked like they were moving smoothly, so he headed out back for a smoke break.

"Hey Ho!" JJ looked at the horse and wagon heading out from the farm he was walking past. It was Robert and his two oldest sons. JJ waved in response.

The cart pulled up beside JJ, and Robert called out, "Ride to the poker game? Sure beats walkin'!" JJ gave a slight nod and climbed into the back of the wagon.

One of the boys, knowing he was a trapper, asked, "Good day for trapping?"

JJ responded, "More of a hunting day, really, and chores."

The boy nodded. "Always chores to do."

JJ looked at the necklace Farm Boy was wearing. "Cougar teeth?"

Farm Boy nodded. "They're something, ain't they! Look at the size of 'em," he exclaimed, holding them aloft. He decided not to share that it was actually his sister's necklace.

They both returned to looking out across the prairie as the wagon creaked and bumped its way up the trail.

Two of Lacy's friends were standing on the second-floor balcony watching the various patrons starting to fill up the saloon. One turned to the other and asked, "You know those three fancy men who came here today? The ones in blue suits?"

The other nodded.

"Well, I decided to check out that train car they came on."

The other turned to face her and said, "You did? How?"

"Well, I noticed that the porter from the train car was here with the horse 'n' carriage. So I walked over towards the station. They had parked the train car behind the station."

"Yeah, but Claude?"

"Claude was gabbing, *blah blah blah*." She made talking movements with her hand. "With the guy in the tower."

"That sounds like Claude."

"So I snuck over behind the station and up to the train car. I went up the back and tried the door. It was unlocked."

"You didn't!"

"I did! And I went inside, and I am telling you, it was the finest, nicest train car I have ever seen. The walls were all polished hardwood, the curtains thick and tasselled, and the chairs were stuffed twice as high as ours, with rich red fabric. I sat in one and sank right down. So comfortable!"

"Pretty fancy!"

"It was! All the lamps had covers on them that looked like stained glass, and there were bookshelves with deep-brown, leather-covered books with gold lettering. On one of them was a crystal decanter with some of the richest brandy I have ever smelled."

"Did you take some?"

"No! I am not a thief!" she bristled at the suggestion.

"Okay, okay, continue."

"So, there were a couple of bedrooms that were so plush and comfy looking, and a bathroom with a tiny, shiny porcelain sink and gold taps. Above it was a mirror with a gold frame. I thought, I could get used to being treated like this."

Her friend nodded in enthusiastic agreement. "What else, what else?"

"Oh, the back of the car was pretty boring, it had a huge polished hardwood table with a dozen fancy chairs around it. I got out of there as quick as I could. I don't think anyone saw me."

They both turned back to watching the patrons filling the bar.

Maddie looked up at her husband. He had been distant and distracted all day.

"Lots to think about?"

George replied, "*So* much. It's not that I don't think I can do it, you know, keep up with the additional demand and meet the deadlines, it's just *so much* to think about. So many pieces to sort out and have lined up." George sighed and his shoulders drooped.

"I sometimes feel the same way about the paper. I mean, it's great that I am selling them to Yorktown now, and I have more people wanting to advertise than I have the space for, But there is more and more work to getting it done on time, and more and more people to please." Maddie smiled a little. "But at least we are the ones steering the wagon. Would still much rather have it this way than doing some repetitive job, the same every day, with someone else in charge."

"True, true," said George.

Still on the topic of selling papers, Maddie said, "I want to write a story about you catching Mr. Muces for the paper. I think it's just the kind of story people like to read about. You know, a potential theft being spoiled and his ridiculous escape attempt. People love a good comeuppance. I am going to change the names of the people involved, I don't want this blowing up into something it isn't. But I do think it is a story worth telling."

"Oh sure, sure," said George. "I mean, everyone in this town knows who you are talking about anyway. But I think your stories about rural life are what is helping sell the paper in Yorktown."

Maddie replied, "Say, isn't it poker Thursday tonight, just what you need to give your mind a rest from all this?"

George's face lit up. "Maddie, in all the madness, I completely forgot—you are so right! I have to head out soon!"

Maddie grabbed George's jacket and gave it to him. "Good luck!" she said, patting his backside as he walked out the door.

The saloon continued to fill as Lacy's friends watched from above. John walked up the stairs, looked shyly with a brief nervous smile at the two women, and disappeared into Room 3.

"What do you think of John?" asked one of the women.

"Uhm. I don't?" replied the other.

"Because a couple of weeks ago, we… uh… you know."

"What, John? Really? For free?"

"No, not for free of course. He did get an, uh, employee discount…"

The first woman covered her mouth to hide a quick snicker. "Why John of all people?"

"Well, he is kind of cute, and shy. I was bored and flirted with him a bit. He was so awkward! I thought it was funny. So I led him by the hand up to Room One, and I have to tell you, it was so sweet! He was so gentle, and caring, and considerate. Such a change from…" she shrugged. "The usual. His wooden teeth took a little getting used to, but it was nice to be, I don't know, treasured for a bit. And it must have been half an hour or so, before, well…"

"Sure, sure. I can… kind of… see that." The din of the nearly full establishment below them grew louder.

They watched as the enormous figure of Brad worked his way through the crowd. "Have you ever?" asked one nudging the other. "Being with that man would be like sleeping with a Grizzly!"

"Brad? No. I mean, I have flirted with him a couple of times, or tried to. I have never seen him with anyone in all the years I have lived here so thought it would be easy. But... nothing."

A door behind them opened and Lacy walked out, done up to her usual high standard.

She smiled at her two friends. One of them said, "Looks like a busy night, Lacy! What are you hoping for?"

Lacy turned to them and said, "A half-dozen men, all who pay up front, hung like rabbits, who last less than thirty seconds."

Lacy swept down the stairs to the main level with her usual grandiosity.

Robert pulled his wagon up in front of Service Mercantile, and tied his horse to the hitching post there. The three passengers clambered out, and all headed towards the saloon.

They could hear the clamour from inside. Robert turned to his oldest son. "Sounds like a busy night. Get a good seat while you can!"

They pushed through the swinging doors at the front of the saloon. The air was thick with smoke, whiskey and beer smell, and a three-piece band was warming up at the far end. And it was packed, a line-up was at the bar, and the various dealers were weaving their way through the crowd to the poker tables, change boxes in hand.

The growth of poker night meant that a lot more of the patrons (mostly men) were not familiar to the locals. A table with mostly locals did form, but it was filled up quickly.

When George walked into the saloon, he was taken aback by the quantity of patrons. His eyesight made it difficult to see a spot at a distance. After walking around the front and seeing no seats, he quickly moved to the back of the room, finding one of the last ones. He sat down at the table and nodded at the others. "Gentlemen," he said. A couple of the others nodded in return.

Robert sat at his usual high-roller table. A couple of well-dressed businessmen were also seated at his table. He thought, *I hope they brought lots of money.*

Pete and Kat were kept busy behind the bar with beer and whiskey, the patrons anxious to get a drink before the poker started. One stranger leaned into Pete and said, "Can I ask you a couple of questions, sir?"

Pete looked at the man, and looked at the crush of patrons at the bar. He said, "Not a good time right now. Come back and ask when it's not quite so busy. The man slid a quarter across the bar. "Whiskey." Pete grabbed a shot of whiskey from under the bar and put it in front of the man. The man waited a moment. "No change?"

Pete replied, "I can either water it down and charge less, or give you pure whiskey. Most of us want the good stuff. Beer is fifteen cents."

The man nodded, not looking convinced, and slammed the shot down. He slid the glass back across the bar where Pete caught it and put it in the dirty-glass box. Pete shouted, "Next!"

Pete quickly took care of five or more customers, then looked around the saloon. All poker tables looked full, and the dealers were finishing up giving change. Pete shouted, "Let's get the cards in the air and play some poker!" He pointed at the band, who immediately started playing. The building chatter quieted down and antes clinked onto the tables.

He started wiping the bar down to soak up the mix of spilled drinks when he was again approached by the stranger. Pete looked at Kathy; she was able to handle the drink orders now that the games had started. "What can I do for you?"

"My name is Deryk Drudge," the man said, extending his arm. Pete shook his hand and replied, "Pete; some call me Sticky Pete."

"Well, Pete, I have a problem that I am hoping you can help me with."

Pete shrugged noncommittally.

"My brother, Mike Drudge went missing almost two years ago. I have been looking for him in Yorktown for the last year or so; he never missed his Saturday beers with me until he suddenly stopped coming. So... something seems off. I did by chance have a conversation with a gentleman who said he knew of him, and heard he was coming here because there were some soft poker games."

"Sure," said Pete.

"So I am wondering if you know whether he has played any poker here?"

Pete thought for a moment, then said, "What did he look like, we get a lot of folks through here. Especially poker night."

Deryk responded. "Well, a lot like me. Black hair, black beard, same Drudge smile."

Pete thought for a moment. "No, not ringing any bells. I have hundreds of people go through this place so that doesn't mean he wasn't here. You could ask some of the poker players here about him, but don't do it until the breaks. We take one every hour."

Deryk looked frustrated, but nodded. "Whiskey," he said, sliding another quarter along the bar.

Four more whiskeys and two beers later, Deryk watched Pete pull out his pocket watch and flip open the cover. He looked at the band until one of the members noticed his eye contact. He pointed at the band and they finished up the song. He closed his pocket watch with a snap and yelled "LAST HAND BEFORE BREAK. TEN MINUTES ONLY, FOLKS!"

There was an immediate shuffle of the players to the veranda and back alley; Deryk walked over to one of the tables and started talking with some of the players.

Pete and Kat were kept busy with the break drink rush.

Pete took a quick look at his watch and was momentarily distracted by loud female laughter. He looked over at the high-roller table and saw Lacy and one of her friends sitting on two men's knees. Pete chuckled to himself and shouted out, "BREAK'S OVER! BREAK'S OVER!" He looked at the band and they started up again.

Pete dealt with the last of the drink rush and turned to see a dog-faced Deryk up at the bar again.

"No luck?" said Pete.

"Nothing," said Deryk, "No one remembers him."

"I would start with some of the old-timers; they have been playing for years," said Pete.

"How do I know who the old-timers are?"

"You can try Robert. He is over at the high-roller table. Wait until the break though; he doesn't like being interrupted when playing."

Another quarter rolled across the bar. "Whiskey."

Two whiskeys and four beers later, Deryk again watched Pete shout out the break call.

Robert stood up at his table and said, "Quick break," to the men remaining seated. One of the well-dressed businessmen was a fish, an inexperienced poker player that Robert had won two significant pots off of. The second, who was currently being fawned over by Lacy's friend, was a bit tougher. However, the toughest player at the table was a new man who Robert had not played before. He was a shark who had built quite a stack of money in front of him. Robert had learned long ago not to play any players with locations in their name; this one's name was "Texas Slim."

One of Lacy's friends and John were watching the action from the balcony. They didn't say much to each other, but both enjoyed watching all the activity below. The big winners getting louder and drunker. The losers blaming cards and luck and sometimes shuffling outside when their bankrolls ran out. And Lacy working her magic on the high-roller tables.

Robert headed out to the veranda. Not to smoke, but to get some head-clearing fresh air and to talk with local farmers he hadn't seen in a while. He had barely started talking when he was approached by Deryk. Deryk explained his situation in a very drunken, unsteady fashion. Robert considered, and then said, "Nope, doesn't sound familiar. He might not have been playing at the high-roller tables though. I would ask one of the lower-stakes players. JJ over there plays lower stakes." Robert pointed to JJ.

JJ was enjoying a smoke when the same very drunk man with rough beard and hair approached him. The man leaned in close, put his hand on JJ's shoulder, and said, "A moment of your time, friend." JJ hated him already. It didn't matter that JJ actually did remember playing with a man similar in appearance to Deryk, he was not interested in a conversation and wanted it to end as soon as possible. He walked the man to the door of the saloon, pointed out George, and went back to his smoke.

Pete called out the break's end, and most people shuffled back to their tables.

Mr. Service looked up at the bar. George was picking up a beer for him along with his own, and he wondered what was taking him so long. He saw George with the beers getting in an animated conversation with a stranger at the bar. Without warning, George got shoved against the bar and both beers spilled on the floor. Mr. Service stood up immediately and started pushing his way over.

Pete saw the shove and said, "Hey, HEY!" to Deryk. Deryk reached inside his pocket and pulled out a Derringer single-shot pistol and pointed it a George. Pete's eyebrows went up and he grabbed Kat by the arm. He urgently spoke into her ear. "Go get the sheriff! George has had a gun pulled on him!" Kat immediately rushed into the back room, out of the back door, and ran down the street to the Sheriff's Office at top speed.

Mr. Service was the only other bar patron to see the gun, and it stopped him in his tracks. "Shit!" He started moving closer, but at a much more careful pace.

Lacy and John were watching from above the crowd below when John noticed the disturbance at the bar. His body grew rigid and he grasped the railing so tight his knuckles went white. "What's wrong?" said his companion. He said nothing. She looked in the direction of his gaze and exclaimed, "Who would want to hurt George? That man wouldn't hurt a fly!"

Deryk's voice was growing louder, and while most people couldn't see the pistol in George's stomach, they could hear the disturbance and see that George had tears streaming down his face.

John leaned over the balcony. "Deryk!" he yelled. "DERYK!"

Deryk's head cocked slightly as he listened. He pushed the gun into George's side and said, "We're headed up there." George walked hot faced and shaking through the crowd up to the stairs. Mr. Service bravely grabbed Deryk by the shoulder and got a wicked elbow in the face for his efforts, drawing blood and knocking out a couple of teeth.

Deryk snarled, "If you want to see your friend here live, I would suggest backing off!" Deryk and George went up the stairs while Mr. Service and a couple of other interested parties stayed at the bottom. Deryk stayed close enough to George that the pistol was not visible.

Deryk, John and George walked into Room 2, Deryk slammed the door behind him. Pete watched the whole thing without moving his gaze, ignoring the numerous pleas for drinks.

JJ watched George head up the stairs and knew by both men's body position that something was up. He guessed that Deryk either had a knife or gun in George's back. He looked at his cards. "Raise."

The sheriff showed up a few minutes later with Kat and a deputy in tow. He got to the front door of the saloon and pushed his way impatiently to the bar where Pete was. Pete pointed up the stairs and said to the sheriff, "They're in Room Two."

The sheriff asked, "Any gunshots?"

Pete shook his head. "I saw a single-shot Derringer but no shots."

The sheriff looked at the crowd of people in the bar, and looked over at Brad who was sitting just behind him.

"Brad, can you clear the way for us? I need to get up there fast."

Brad stood and pushed his way through the crowd with vigour and power. Some of the people he pushed out of the way looked most perturbed, but thought better of any trouble once they saw the size of Brad and the two men who were following him. The sheriff drew his gun and started up the stairs staying low, followed by his deputy.

The combination of Brad pushing through the crowd and a sheriff with his gun drawn now meant most of the saloon's attention was clearly focused on the unfolding events.

The sheriff moved up the stairs to the outside of Room 2. He stood on one side of the door, while the deputy stood on the other side. The sheriff backed up, and with a dynamic, powerful movement, kicked in the door. He motioned for the deputy to go inside. The deputy did, gun drawn, followed by the sheriff.

The crowd downstairs now mostly stood, captivated by the action upstairs. Mr. Service clenched and unclenched his hands nervously. Brad ensured no one went up the stairs; no one wanted to.

A number of faces that knew George looked concerned. The out-of-towners were riveted by the unfolding drama.

Nothing happened for what seemed like an impossibly long time. No gunshots. No shouting. No sounds of scuffling. Finally, after a good ten minutes or so, Deryk was led out of the room, his hands handcuffed behind his back. The sheriff held him by his cuffs, moving him forward while the deputy followed. They descended the stairs and the crowd obediently parted, letting the party of three pass. Deryk did not look mad or defeated. He looked almost… penitent. They walked out of the front doors and down the street towards the Sheriff's Office.

A few people looked almost disappointed that the action had resolved so peacefully. Then, John burst out of Room 2, and with great haste headed through the crowd and out the front door, following the sheriff.

Mr. Service looked at Brad, and then hurried up the stairs. Brad let him pass. When he looked in the hotel room, he could see George sitting on the side of a bed, hunched over, looking pale and exhausted and still shaking. He walked over to George, who looked up with a drawn and tear-stained face. He looked relieved to see who it was. Mr. Service walked over to the dresser in the hotel room, grabbed two cloths, and soaked both with water from a water jug. He gave one to George who started wiping his face. He used the other to soothe his now-growing fat lip.

"You okay, buddy?" asked George.

"*Me*? Are *you* Okay?" retorted Mr. Service.

"Yeah, that was, a little, unexpected," said George. Mr. Service stood in silence for a moment. George turned to look up at him. "Thanks for always having my back, really… Thanks."

"Oh, of course," replied Mr. Service.

"Now I have to go down and face all those people after... after... crying." said George quietly.

"Are you kidding, buddy?" replied Mr. Service. "If someone had pulled a gun on me, I would have filled my pants on the spot. There I would be, pants full, stinking up the joint. You have nothing to be ashamed of. Believe me."

George took in a deep breath, and stood. Mr. Service said, "You ready?" George nodded.

They walked down the stairs together until just before getting to the bottom. George was very aware of a hundred or so faces looking at him. He paused at the bottom of the stairs and shouted, "Let's play some poker!"

A small cheer lifted from the crowd and the band started up again as they shuffled back to their respective tables. Pete handed George and Mr. Service a beer each on their way by. "On the house," he said, winking.

George sat down at his table and threw in his one-penny ante. The dealer started dealing. A couple of moments later, he felt a strong hand on his shoulder. It was Robert. He leaned into George and spoke quietly. "If you want a ride home, just let me know," he said. "That was a heck of a thing."

George nodded in thanks, and took a look at his cards. Two aces!

Epilogue

GEORGE LOOKED THROUGH the small opening that was the Junction Station ticket office window. He could see Claude hunched over the desk on the other side of the ticket office, looking closely at the train orders for the day.

"Good morning, Claude!" he said.

Claude quickly turned and got up from his desk. "Return ticket to Yorktown, I assume?" George nodded and asked, "And how are you today?"

Claude found the appropriate ticket and passed it to George. He replied, "Not bad. Got five runs coming in from east, three from west, so a busy day today. Plus the usual passenger service." He paused. "Makes the day go by faster. And you?"

George smiled. "Well, got some business to take care of first." He patted the full canvas satchel at his side. "But then, a visit I have been looking forward to for a while."

Claude smiled a rare smile. "Well, happy travels then." George nodded back.

The train was already waiting, steaming and ready, a short one today with just two passenger cars. George stepped up the stairs to the first car and found himself a seat on the Junction side.

He watched as two blurry figures, most likely Pete and John, swept off the veranda of the saloon and put out the chairs. He saw who he assumed was Mr. Service roll two barrels to the front of his store and get one set up for the produce of the day. He watched Lorraine tie Spirit up in front of the print shop, greet Mr. Sneed, and head inside.

The whistle blasted and the train jolted forward. George watched his town go by and quickly turn to country. A steam tractor chuffed and strained its way along the new section of Robert's farm, pulling a wide multi-blade plough creating five neat furrows in the ground behind it. The morning sun cast long shadows on the cows in the next field, making their legs seem ridiculously long.

George let his mind rest, allowing the passing countryside to relax him with its familiar colours and sights.

Pulling into Yorktown, George was surprised at the number of new buildings and changes that had occurred in the year since he had been here. The town stretched a full block farther towards Junction, and had a new brick building with thick black metal pipes and ducts, called Steeple Metalworks.

His first stop on this journey was the small newsstand location at the station. While the train to Junction wasn't typically that busy, the station platform was usually full with passengers travelling the other direction. He carefully counted out ten of the *Junction Herald* and passed them to the newsagent. The newsagent thanked him, and gave him a nickel to pay for the papers.

His next stops were two grocers, both of whom took 20 papers. He chatted with the store owners, not because he felt like chatting, but because he understood the importance of keeping Maddie's business contacts happy. Both provided him with dimes, one tossed it to him casually, directly from the cash register. The other carefully recorded the transaction in a ledger before handing George the dime.

The last stop for the paper run was the newsagent closest to downtown. George had to wait for a bustle of customers in this busiest part of the city before the owner noticed him and waved him forward. He took the papers and said, "You're not Maddie."

George smiled and replied, "No, Maddie's husband, George," and held out his hand. The newsagent shook it and handed over twenty-five cents. "Tell her we love her paper. The country folks around here say it reminds them of home."

"Will do," said George.

His next stop was Smith and Son's Windows. They had also expanded into an adjacent building and George could see two work crews working on prep and assembly in an expanded area.

He walked inside the building and headed up the stairs to the office. He knocked on the door.

"Enter."

He opened the door.

"George, long time!   Let me guess. Five hundred two by twos?"

George chuckled. "Nope, fifty. But, I do want a couple of eight by sixes and some two by eights, along with others. Building a new grocery store in Junction." He slid his order across the desk.

"Thank you, will file this right away and get it out to you in a couple of weeks."

George was impressed. "Two weeks. Pretty good!"

John nodded. "Yep, four shifts a day, two morning, two afternoon. This city keeps growing." John smiled and crossed his arms.

"Thank you sir!" George shook his hand and headed down the stairs.

He walked down the street to the tenement housing block he had stayed in two years earlier. There were two new buildings; this area had expanded as well. The streets were scattered with groups of dirty-faced children, trudging workers and weary horses.

He walked up to the entrance of his friend's building, opened the front door, walked through to the back of the hallway, and knocked on Alex's door.

"Hello?" came a voice from inside.

"Hello!" replied George enthusiastically.

The door opened a tiny crack and a woman's suspicious eye peered through it. It quickly closed again. George could hear rapid conversation inside. Then silence.

"Bad time?" said George to the door. "I can come back later?"

George turned to leave and thought, *Next time I will send a telegram.*

The door behind him opened.

"GEORGE!" George turned to see Alex, a broad smile on his face with arms open.

"Alex!" He walked into the embrace enthusiastically and both men patted each other's backs with vigour.

"Come in!" Alex said. "Sorry for the door, we have to be a bit careful here."

"I should have let you know I was coming. Wasn't thinking," replied George, tapping his head.

Alex smiled. "I am glad you are here. Didn't know if I would see you again." His wife gestured towards the kitchen table and they both sat down.

"Tea?" she asked.

George nodded enthusiastically. "So how have things been going, my friend?"

"The kids are doing well, both in school and reasonably healthy." Alex looked at his wife and she nodded in confirmation. "We are now working two shifts at the factory, so the change in schedule has taken some getting used to. It's either six till four, or four till two a.m. Nothing we can't cope with." Alex again looked at his wife.

"Oh, nothing we can't cope with," she said a hint sarcastically.

"How about you, friend? How's the quick-building business? I have seen a couple of your posters around town; hoped that was you."

"It is, it is," said George. George and Alex talked about the details of his business, the complexities of getting leaks and other things fixed in the tenement building, and challenges of raising kids in the city.

George asked specifically about Alex's pay at the factory. Alex looked down a bit, and then said, "Well, as you know, I was made shift manager a year before you came, and that came with a raise."

"A good raise?" said George.

Alex shook his head slowly and his wife sighed. He said, "Two cents an hour."

"And nothing since?" said George.

Alex kept looking at the floor while his wife looked uncomfortable.

"Forgive me for prying into private matters, but I have a proposition for you, and your family," said George. George stood up and pulled out a chair at the table. He looked at Alex's wife and indicated she should sit down. She did.

"My business has made a sudden leap in growth this spring, and I have a number of projects and a tight timeline on all of them." Alex's wife cocked her head listening and Alex was focused on George.

George continued, "I was very impressed with your organization and running of your shift at the window factory, and frankly"—George tapped his lip—"think you are underpaid. There is a thing happening right now where people with journeyman-level skills are being paid as factory workers, and not being given the chance to apprentice as a journeyman."

Alex's wife nodded with her eyes wide open.

"I am looking for someone who can lead the mill I am setting up to build my quick buildings.

Someone who not only understands wood, but also understands how to lead the team, set up jigs, and stay organized. I think that is something you can do."

Both Alex and his wife looked slightly stunned.

"And, I have two building projects starting basically next week. One is a new grocery store, and one is a new dedicated workshop and storage building on my property. And I would really like to have you be part of that as well."

Alex was nodding slowly.

His wife replied with a stammering voice. "He can't do part-time projects; we need reliable work, and I need his help around here. He can't be away for long times." She shook her head vigorously.

"Here is what I am offering," continued George. "Starting next week, full-time work. Permanent. As an apprentice to getting your journeyman, Alex. You and your wife"—George looked at Alex's wife who was looking a bit shocked—"will have to decide what to do about living arrangements. I can offer some temporary land and one of my buildings as a living space until you decide something more permanent. We do have a school in Junction, and from what I have heard, it is a good school."

George looked at both of them; they both looked frozen.

"I know this is a lot. This is a big decision for you. But I would be honoured to have you come and work for me, Alex. I am offering you a wage five cents higher per hour than you get at the factory to start, and once you get your apprenticeship finished, you can earn a full journeyman's wage."

Alex's eyebrows went up. His wife remained stiff and wide-eyed.

George looked at both of them for an uncomfortable moment, and took a sip of his tea. He waited and took a few more sips over time.

Alex and his wife sat unmoving for a while, but no questions. Eventually Alex said, "Thank you very much for your generous offer." But nothing more.

George stood. "Thank you for the tea," he said to Alex's wife. "I know this is a huge decision for you, and a big change. Moving from a city to a small town is a big decision." Both people remained sitting unmoved. "I would love to give you more time, but I am getting started next week on these projects, so need someone fairly soon. If you could let me know by Friday, then I can know what I am going to do next. For help."

He again looked at the couple and bowed slightly. "Thank you very much for the hospitality. I hope to see you again, even if your answer is no. I consider you both friends."

Alex stood up and led George to the door. "Thank you," he said. "Thank you, I..." and said nothing more.

George smiled what he hoped was a reassuring smile. "I hope to hear from you by Friday." Alex closed the door.

George stood by the closed door and thought for a moment: *Somehow I pictured that differently.*

JJ woke that morning feeling like something was wrong. His stomach was tense, his back clenched, his jaw tight. He felt as if he was urgently late for something, or that he should be somewhere that he wasn't.

He got out of bed and put on the minimum of clothes necessary to go outside in the spring air. He put on his leather shoes, the ones he normally used for climbing. He didn't put on a pack, bring a gun, or even put a snack in his pocket.

He swept out of his cabin and down beside the river without closing the door behind him, the cool air fuelling his motion.

He needed to move, he needed to find; he needed to feed the restlessness.

His body moved at high speed up the Blue River. He easily jumped over fallen logs, or without breaking stride, ducked under them. His navigation required no thought; his experience moved him. He made no mistakes in his quest for motion.

Occasionally he would burst through a thicket at pace, raising his arms in front of him to protect his face. He would crack through, sending branches and astonished birds all directions, continuing unabated through the woods.

Escaping.

When the Blue River curved to the left, he continued straight, ignoring his usual path and moving rapidly through the forest, without following paths or trails, feeling the ground through the soles of his shoes and allowing it to inform his motion.

He moved through deciduous forest. Grand maples, thin, bending poplars, and light-barked aspens. He did not notice the spring flowers pushing through. He did not notice the first couple of pine trees, thin and branches sparse in their race to the sun.

He covered more distance in two hours than he usually covered in a day. His running was frustration turned to movement.

The forest changed from the green and humidity of the leafed trees to the dark green and dryness of a coniferous forest. The spiky pines with their grey bark pushed towards the sky. He pushed past long-needled pines, their scaly bark cracking to reveal brown interiors.

Anticipating.

He finally slowed, his heart pounding its pulse in his head, his mouth thick and throat dry. He looked at the forest floor. It had changed from the explosion of life of the deciduous forest to a dry brown needle-covered surface. Any logs on the forest floor were covered with a thick layer of moss that gave way to any weight.

It was dark, dry and quiet. There was no breeze moving the branches, no squirrels or birds breaking the silence.

Waiting.

He walked lightly without sound until he noticed a white trunk, stark in its comparison with the greys and black-browns that surrounded it.

It was a white birch, and it looked so completely out of place that JJ was captured by it. He walked up and touched its smooth white bark, paper-white curls floating down as he ran his hand up the surface. He had never seen a birch with such perfect bark; he reached high and then allowed his gaze to continue up the tree.

As he looked towards the canopy, he froze. The hairs on his arm stood on end, and his heart beat irregularly. The top of the tree was entirely clad in the brightest yellow leaves he had ever seen, brighter than even the poplars of the area in fall.

The sun filtering through the bright leaves gave them a glow, a glow that left him mesmerized.

A single leaf broke free from its branch, and floated down as JJ watched it, spiralling and sweeping back and forth before gently alighting on the ground.

He looked up, and saw another two leaves break free, taking their long and random route down. Not a breeze stirred, not a bird moved, not a squirrel twitched.

Three or four leaves started their long journey down, one just touching his forehead with a dry and cool touch before falling beside him.

He was without thoughts, without reason as he stepped back a few paces from the tree. He untucked and unbuttoned his shirt, rolling it off his shoulders with a single motion and allowing it to fall from his fingertips to the forest floor below.

More and more leaves started to fall from the tree, filling the air with yellow streaks and falling to the forest floor with a quiet, constant patter.

JJ sank to his knees and raised his hands skyward as the leaves started falling thickly, touching his head and face, bouncing lightly off his shoulders, and rolling down his chest.

He put his face in his hands. The leaves gently touched and rolled down his back. Tears came from his eyes, down his cheeks, through his fingers and down the front of his forearms. They dropped off his elbows to join the leaves below.

Acknowledgements

To my wife, whose compassion, patience, and carefully worded advice made this book possible.

To my daughter for bringing light and love into my life.

To my mother, who taught me compassion and patience, and has always encouraged my story telling.

To my father and Lani, who have always been there for me, through thick and thin.

To my ever-supportive brothers.

And a huge thank you to Terry, my editor, who taught me that an exclamation mark is just as effective as sentences in ALL CAPS, how to spell 'Okay,' and who taught me how to punctuate quotations and about consistency of character.

To my publisher, Pete, who has crafted this into a book for me, who taught me about adverbs, pacing, and consistency of voice.

And to my friends and coworkers, some of whom I literally owe my life.